A delicious warmth spr
when he deepened the

"I think we'd better...stop this before I do something that's sure to...get me into big trouble," Nate said, sounding as short of breath as she felt. "Right now, I want you more than I want my next breath, and as bad as I hate to say this, it might be best for you to sleep across the hall tonight."

The warmth inside her increased and her pulse raced. "Is that what you want me to do?"

"Hell, no!" He laughed as he shook his head. "What I'd like to do is to take you upstairs right now, remove every stitch of your clothes and spend the entire night making love to every inch of your delightful body."

Her heart skipped a beat and she had to remind herself to breathe. "Then why don't you?" she asked before she could stop herself.

A deep groan rumbled up from his chest. "Jessie, I'm not in any shape right now to be a gentleman. If you don't mean what you just said, then it would be a real good idea to put some distance between us right about now."

Reaching up, she cupped his lean cheeks with her hands. "I don't want to move away from you, Nate."

* * *

Pregnant with the Rancher's Baby is part of The Good, the Bad and the Texan series—Running with these billionaires will be one wild ride

Dear Reader,

I just love stories where a "love 'em and leave 'em" type of guy meets that one woman he just can't walk away from. Oh, he might try when things seem to be getting a little more serious than he's comfortable with. But something always keeps drawing him back to her. What he doesn't realize is that he's found the love of his life. He'll try to deny it, make excuses for it and even do his best to outrun it, but in the end, he'll gladly give in and admit that he loves her and can't live without her.

The fifth installment of The Good, the Bad and the Texan series, *Pregnant with the Rancher's Baby*, finds rodeo cowboy Nate Rafferty learning that lesson the hard way. Jessie Farrell is tired of Nate's games and only tells him that she's pregnant with his baby because she feels he has the right to know he's fathered a child. But is it too late for him to convince her that he wants her in his life, as well as their child?

Sometimes rocky and filled with potholes, the road to love isn't always easy, but it's always worth the journey. So please sit back and enjoy the ride as we find out what happens when a playboy of the rodeo circuit finds that what he's been running from all this time is the very thing he's always wanted.

All the best,

Kathie DeNosky

PREGNANT WITH THE RANCHER'S BABY

KATHIE DENOSKY

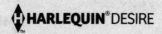

ISBN-13: 978-0-373-73424-5

Pregnant with the Rancher's Baby

Copyright © 2015 by Kathie DeNosky

Reclaimed by the Rancher
Copyright © 2015 by Harlequin Books S.A.

The publisher acknowledges Janice Maynard for her contribution to *Reclaimed by the Rancher*.

Recycling programs for this product may not exist in your area.

Printed in U.S.A.

www.Harlequin.com

CONTENTS

Kathie DeNosky lives in her native southern Illinois on the land her family settled in 1839. She writes highly sensual stories with a generous amount of humor. Her books have appeared on the *USA TODAY* bestseller list and received numerous awards, including two National Readers' Choice Awards. Kathie enjoys going to rodeos, traveling to research settings for her books and listening to country music. Readers may contact her by emailing kathie@kathiedenosky.com. They can also visit her website, kathiedenosky.com, or find her on Facebook.

Books by Kathie DeNosky

HARLEQUIN DESIRE

Texas Cattleman's Club: After the Storm

For His Brother's Wife

The Good, the Bad and the Texan

His Marriage to Remember
A Baby Between Friends
Your Ranch...Or Mine?
The Cowboy's Way
Pregnant with the Rancher's Baby

Visit the Author Profile page at Harlequin.com, or kathiedenosky.com, for more titles.

PREGNANT WITH THE RANCHER'S BABY

Kathie DeNosky

This book is dedicated to my beautiful daughter,
Angela DeNosky Blumenstock.
Thank you for the research help
and for being the sweetest daughter
a mother could ever ask for.

One

Nate Rafferty couldn't help but smile as he looked around the big, open area in one of his newly constructed barns. From the minute he'd mentioned having a party to celebrate his buying and renovating the Twin Oaks Ranch, his brothers' wives had decided it needed to be a theme party. He'd been fine with that and told his sisters-in-law they were in charge of making it happen.

He'd even left the decision up to the women on what the theme would be, and they had outdone themselves, turning what was going to be his hay barn into a kid-friendly haunted house and full-on Halloween party. The monsters, scarecrows and ghosts were cute rather than scary, and his niece and nephews were going to love all the pumpkins, happy jack-o'-lanterns and garlands of colorful fall leaves that had been hung around the dance floor and bandstand.

Trying to decide if he wanted to go as the Lone Ranger or John Wayne, Nate walked out of the barn and started across the ranch yard toward the house. He'd gone only a few feet when he stopped dead in his tracks. A petite blond-haired woman was just getting out of the gray compact SUV she'd parked close to the garage.

How in the name of Sam Hill had she found him? And why?

He'd purposely avoided mentioning anything about buying the Twin Oaks Ranch to Jessica Farrell. He'd planned to wait until he finished renovating it, so he could surprise her and invite her to spend a weekend with him. Of course, the last time he'd seen her had been about four and a half months back—when she had still been speaking to him.

Not that he'd been all that worried about it. He had never had a problem charming his way back into her good graces and he had no reason to believe he couldn't do so again, even though she'd been pretty determined that their on-again, off-again relationship was permanently off.

It had been that way between them for the past couple of years and whenever it seemed like things were getting a little too serious, he always found a reason to break things off between them. But the last time she'd told him not to bother calling her again and to forget where she lived.

Of course, it wasn't the first time she'd told him to

lose her phone number. They went through something similar about every three or four months. He'd give her time to simmer down, call and sweet-talk her into seeing him again. Then, after spending several weeks of being real cozy with her, he could feel himself start to get in a little deeper than he intended. That's when he'd cut and run.

He knew it wasn't fair to Jessie. She was a wonderful woman and deserved better than the likes of him. But where she was concerned, he didn't seem to have a choice. He simply couldn't stay away from her.

But this was the first time she'd sought *him* out and he couldn't for the life of him figure out why, especially not after the way they'd ended things the last time. When they'd parted several months ago, it had been different than before. He'd told her that he thought they should take a break and stop seeing each other for a while. That's when he had seen a finality in her violet eyes that hadn't been there before. But she was here now, so it must not have been all that final.

"Jessie, it's good to see you again," he said, walking toward her. Dressed in jeans and an oversized pink sweatshirt, she somehow managed to make the baggy fleece look sexy. Real sexy. "It's been a while, darlin'. How have you been?"

When she turned to face him, she didn't look all that happy to see him. "Do you have a few minutes?" she asked, her tone serious. "I need to talk to you."

"Sure." He couldn't imagine what she wanted to talk about, but at the moment, he didn't care. He wasn't going to tell her, but the truth was, he had missed her—

missed the sound of her soft voice and her sweet smile. "Why don't we go inside and catch up?"

Her long ponytail swayed back and forth as she shook her head. "I won't be here that long."

Placing his arm around her slender shoulders, he turned her toward the house. "You didn't drive all the way from Waco just to turn around and go back," he said as he ushered her across the patio to the French doors. "I'll tell my housekeeper you'll be staying for supper."

When they entered the family room, she surprised him when she ducked from beneath his arm and turned to face him. "Don't bother, Nate. I worked the late shift last night and as soon as we talk, I need to get back home and get some sleep." She was a registered professional nurse he'd met when she had taken care of his brother a couple of years ago after Sam had been injured in a rodeo accident.

"You can always sleep here," he said, grinning.

If looks could kill, he would have been a dead man in two seconds flat. "You have a housekeeper?" she asked. When he nodded, she frowned as she looked around. "Is there somewhere a little more private where we can talk?"

Nate stared at her. He'd never seen her as determined as she appeared to be at that moment. "Let's go into my office," he finally said, motioning toward the arched doorway leading out into the foyer. "We can talk privately in there."

Guiding her along, he waited until they were seated in his office with the door closed. "What was it you needed to talk to me about?" he asked, looking across the desk at her sitting in the leather armchair in front of him.

She nibbled on her lower lip as she stared down at her tightly clasped hands resting in her lap. "I want you to know that it's taken me over four months to come to the decision to tell you." When she looked directly at him, her pretty violet eyes were filled with resignation. "My first inclination was not to bother. But I didn't think that would be fair to you."

Nate sat up straight in his desk chair as his scalp started to tingle. He wasn't sure what she was talking about, but his gut was telling him that whatever she had to say would be life changing. Had she met someone else? Was she telling him that she had committed herself to another man and it wasn't fair not to tell him? Or was she talking about something else?

"Why don't you stop beating around the bush and just tell me what you think I need to hear?" he asked.

She took a deep breath and met his questioning gaze head on. "I'm almost five months pregnant."

"You're pregnant," he repeated. His gaze flew to her stomach as her words began to sink in and it felt like the air had suddenly been sucked out of the room. His heart raced and his knees threatened to buckle as he stood up and came around the desk to stand in front of her. "You're going to have a baby?"

"That's what pregnant means."

"How did that happen?" he asked before he could stop himself.

The look she gave him stated louder than words that

she had some serious doubts about the level of his intelligence. "If you don't know about the birds and bees by now, Nate, you never will."

Taking a deep breath, he shook his head in an effort to clear the ringing in his ears. "You know what I mean." He rubbed the sudden tension building at the base of his neck. "We were always careful about protection."

"There could have been a microscopic tear in one of the condoms or some other kind of defect." She shrugged one slender shoulder. "Whatever happened, I'm pregnant and you're the daddy. But I don't want anything from you," she added hurriedly. "I make more than enough to support myself and the baby, and I'm perfectly capable of raising a child on my own. I just thought it was only fair to let you know about the baby and find out if you want to be part of his or her life. If not, I want you to sign all of your rights over to me and we'll both be out of your life for good."

"Like hell," he said emphatically. "If I have a kid, I'm going to be involved in every aspect of its life."

She gave him a short nod, then stood up. "That's all I wanted to know. I'll have my attorney get in touch with yours. They can work out a fair custody agreement and a suitable visitation schedule."

"Where are you going?" he asked, reaching out to place his hands on her shoulders to stop her. "You can't just waltz in here, tell me that you're having my baby and then leave."

"Yes, I can," she said. There was a defiance in her voice that warned him not to argue with her. "If I didn't have a conscience, I wouldn't even be here. But I happen to believe that a man has a right to know when he's fathered a child, even if he's not dependable. For now, that's really all you need to know."

A strong sense of guilt settled across his shoulders. Given their past and the way he'd treated her and their relationship, he should probably be grateful that she had bothered telling him at all. But he couldn't let her leave without discussing things further. There were things he wanted—needed—to know.

"Jessie, I'm sorry for the way things have been between us in the past," he said, meaning it. "I take full responsibility for that and if I could go back and change it, I would. Unfortunately, I can't do that. But from here on out it's important that we work together."

She backed away from him. "I told you I won't keep you from seeing the baby. The lawyers will—"

"Yeah, I got that," he interrupted. He took a deep breath. "Look, I realize that I'm not exactly your favorite person right now and I can't say I blame you. But there are things I want to discuss with you and a whole hell of a lot more that we need to decide."

She stared at him for a moment before she spoke again. "I'm sure this came as a shock. Believe me, I wasn't expecting it either. But it doesn't have to be complicated. We can let the lawyers take care of sorting all of this out."

"Darlin', I don't see how this can be anything but complicated," he said, noticing for the first time how tired she looked. A sudden idea began to take shape as he stared into her pretty violet eyes. "You're exhausted. Why don't we table this for the time being?"

"Don't worry about me," she said, shrugging. "I'll be fine as soon as I go home and get some sleep."

"I don't like the idea of you driving all the way back to Waco as tired as you are," he said. "It isn't safe."

"I'll be okay." She frowned. "Besides, my welfare isn't any of your concern."

"Yes, it is," he insisted. "Do you have to work tonight?"

She shook her head. "I have the weekend off. Why?"

"My family is having a Halloween party here tomorrow night and I'd really like for you to join us. I've got five guest bedrooms upstairs and you can have your pick of any of them." He used his index finger to brush a strand of blond hair that had escaped her ponytail from her smooth cheek as an excuse to touch her. His finger tingled from the contact and he was heartened by the slight widening of her pretty eyes, indicating that she felt it, too. "It will also give us time to talk and make a few decisions after you've had time to rest."

He'd wisely avoided mentioning that she could share the master suite with him. He might not be the brightest bulb in the chandelier, but he wasn't fool enough to think she would be receptive to picking up their relationship where they left it almost five months ago.

She tried to hide a yawn behind her small, delicate hand. "I told you the law—"

"I know. But don't you think it would save a lot of time and be easier for all concerned if we had everything worked out in advance?" he asked.

"Nate, I'm really too tired to discuss this right now," she said, yawning. "All I want is to get home and go to bed."

"At least take a nap before you start back to Waco," he stalled. If he could get her to stay for a while, it would give him time to come to grips with the unbelievable fact that he was going to be a daddy. At the moment he was completely numb. But he needed to pull it together so he could think. He had to come up with a better argument for her staying, at least for the party. Now that he knew she was carrying his baby, it was even more important that they work things out. And damned quick.

"Maybe just a short power nap would help," she conceded.

Without hesitation, he put his arm around her shoulders to guide her out into the foyer and up the stairs. He wasn't going to give her time to change her mind.

When he walked her down the upstairs hall, Nate opened the door to the bedroom across from his. "Will this room be all right?"

"I'm leaving as soon as I wake up," she warned.

"Just get some sleep now," he said, leading her over to the bed. Pulling back the colorful quilt, he waited until she kicked off her tennis shoes and got into bed before he bent down to kiss her forehead. "If you need anything, I'll be in my office."

She had already fallen asleep.

Standing beside the bed, he stared down at the only woman he hadn't been able to stay away from. Jessie was smart, funny and as sweet as she was pretty. So why hadn't he been able to commit to her?

Nate knew his foster brother Lane Donaldson would probably have a field day using his master's degree in psychology to analyze Nate's motives. But Nate didn't want to delve too deeply into his reasons for avoiding commitments. It all tied into his past and it wasn't something he could change, nor was he eager to think about that dark time in his life.

The only thing he could do now was what his foster father Hank Calvert would expect of any of the boys he finished raising. Hank had preached to them over and over that when a man makes the decision to sleep with a woman, he'd better be ready to accept his responsibilities if he made her pregnant. And that was just what Nate intended to do.

His aversion to commitment was about to undergo a dramatic change. Jessie had shown up to tell him he was going to be a daddy and he fully intended to do right by her and his kid. Sometime within the next week, he was going to kiss his blissful bachelorhood goodbye and make her his wife.

When Jessie woke up, bright sunlight peeked through a part in the yellow calico curtains and it took a moment for her to realize where she was.

After working all night in the traumatic brain injury ICU, she had called Nate's brother Sam to ask where she could find Nate. She hated having to involve Sam in her quest to get hold of Nate, but Nate had moved recently. The last time he had broken things off between them, she had deleted his number from her cell. Sam had been very nice and given her directions to the Twin Oaks Ranch. She supposed she could have asked for Nate's number and called, but news like hers was something that needed to be delivered in person.

After going to her prenatal checkup, she had driven directly to the ranch to tell Nate he was the father of her baby. In hindsight, she probably should have gotten some sleep before she confronted him with the news. But if she had put it off any longer, she couldn't be certain she wouldn't have talked herself out of telling him at all.

For the past few months, she'd been torn over what to do and she still wasn't certain she had made the right choice in telling him about the baby. For one thing, she was beyond tired of being Nate's puppet. In the past, he would give her a call and talk her into rekindling their relationship, then when everything seemed to be going great between them, he'd find a reason they should stop seeing each other for a while. And for another, she wasn't sure he deserved to have equal custody of the baby. How good of a father would he be, given his inclination for coming and going the way he'd done in the past?

The last time he decided to pull his vanishing act, she'd told him not to bother getting in touch with her again. It had broken her heart, but she refused to allow him to control the course of their relationship any longer. Shortly after that she had discovered she was pregnant. And even though she felt it was only right to let a man know he had fathered a child, her main concern was whether or not Nate would always be there for the baby. It was one thing to disappoint her. It was something else entirely if he disappointed their child.

Unsettled by the thought, she threw back the covers to sit up on the side of the bed. That's when she realized just how exhausted she'd been. She had not only slept the rest of yesterday and last night, she was still fully dressed.

Jessie quickly made the bed and headed downstairs. She had the next two nights off and she needed to get home. There were several things she needed to get done this weekend and she still had an hour's drive just to get back to Waco.

As she reached the bottom of the stairs, she sighed heavily when Nate came out of the office. So much for avoiding him on her way out.

"Good morning, sleepyhead," he said cheerfully.

Why did the man have to look so darned good to her? She didn't want to notice how his straight light brown hair stylishly brushed the collar of his chambray shirt or the way his blue eyes twinkled when he smiled at her. She was still angry with him and resented the way he thought he could come and go in her life without a second thought to the effect it had on her—how much it hurt her emotionally.

"You should have awakened me," she said, noticing the grandfather clock in the foyer indicated it was already midmorning.

"You were tired." His smile turned to a grin. "Besides, I thought you'd probably want to be fully rested for the party tonight."

"I'm not attending your party," she said, stepping down onto the cream-colored marble tile floor of the foyer. "I told you that yesterday."

He shook his head as he walked over to her. "No, you didn't."

"It was implied and you know it," she stated. "When you insisted that I had to get some sleep before I drove home, I told you I intended to leave as soon as I woke up from a nap. That was a strong indication that I had no intention of attending your family gathering."

He reached out to lightly run his finger along her jaw, causing her skin to tingle where he touched her. "Now that you've had some rest, would you like a cup of coffee or something to eat?" he asked, ignoring her argument against staying for his party. "I don't know all that much about pregnancy, but when they were expecting, all of my sisters-in-law ate like ranch hands once they got past being sick."

"I cut out caffeine when I discovered I was pregnant, but a muffin or bagel and a glass of milk would be appreciated," she answered, knowing just what the women had gone through.

In the early weeks of her pregnancy, just the thought of food was enough to make her sick. But now that the morning sickness had cleared up, it seemed she was hungry all of the time.

"Why don't you have a seat in my office and I'll go tell my housekeeper to fix a tray for you," he said, placing his hand to her back to guide her toward the doorway.

"Why don't I eat in the kitchen and then just go out

the back door to my car when I'm done?" she countered, starting to turn in the opposite direction of the office.

"We have to talk," he insisted, bringing his arm up to wrap around her shoulders and steer her back toward his office.

"Nate, it would be better to let the lawyers—"

"Do you really want strangers calling the shots on how we go about raising our kid?" he interrupted.

Jessie stared at him as she tried to decide what to do. He had a point about attorneys sitting across a conference table making the important decisions about their child. It really did seem impersonal and detached from the situation. But she had wanted to avoid spending any more time with him than she had to. For the past two and a half years Nate Rafferty had been her biggest weakness and she needed to stay strong in order to resist his charming appeal.

"I only have two nights off and I have things I want to accomplish," she hedged. She had intended to start cleaning out the second bedroom in her apartment to turn it into a nursery.

"This is the future of our baby, Jessie." The earnest expression on his handsome face made her feel guilty and she found herself nodding in agreement in spite of her need to put distance between them.

Fifteen minutes later, Jessie stared at the small bowl of fresh fruit, a honey-wheat bagel with cream cheese, scrambled eggs, crispy bacon, a glass of orange juice and a tall glass of milk sitting on a tray on the edge of Nate's desk. "Whose army were you intending to feed?" she asked. "I can't eat all of this."

"Rosemary said you needed the protein and fruit as well as the calcium in the milk and vitamin C from the orange juice," he said, shrugging as he lowered himself into the armchair beside her. "She said it would be good for both you and the baby."

Jessie's eyes widened. "You told your housekeeper I'm pregnant?"

He nodded. "She has six kids and fifteen grandkids. They're all healthy and I figured if anyone would know what your nutritional needs are now that you're pregnant, she would."

While she appreciated his thoughtfulness, Jessie wasn't entirely certain she was comfortable with him telling others about the baby until they had worked out an agreement they could both live with. But she wasn't going to argue with him about it now. They had bigger issues to settle.

"You said you wanted to work out custody and visitation?" she asked, picking up the fork on the tray to take a bite of the fluffy scrambled eggs.

He shook his head, then took a deep breath as if what he was about to say was extremely difficult for him. "None of that will be necessary once we're married."

She stopped with the fork halfway to her mouth. "Excuse me?"

"We'll do the right thing and get married," he repeated as if it was the answer to all of their problems.

Her appetite deserting her, Jessie slowly placed the

fork full of eggs back on the plate and shook her head. "No, we won't."

"Sure we will," he said, reaching to take her hand in his. "I've already qualified for the National Finals. I'll skip the rodeo this coming weekend and we can have the wedding here. Or if you prefer, we can fly to Vegas and have a reception for family and friends at a later date."

Jerking her hand from his, she stood up to pace the length of the room. "Have you lost your ever-loving mind? I'm not going to marry you."

He rose to his feet and, walking over to her, placed his hands on her shoulders to stare down at her from his much taller height. "I didn't mean to upset you, darlin'. I'm pretty sure it's not good for you or the baby."

"How would you know?" she demanded, glaring up into his incredible blue eyes. "How many times have you been pregnant?"

He gave her a sheepish grin. "This is a first for both of us."

"Never mind. It doesn't matter. You wouldn't get the point, even if I explained it to you." She shook her head. "I didn't come here to tell you that I'm having a baby because I wanted you to marry me. I simply thought you should know that you'd fathered a child. Period. If you want to be part of the baby's life, I won't try to stop you. But I'm not part of the deal, Nate. We can work something out so that we're both involved with raising this baby, but that doesn't mean we'll be involved with each other."

He took a deep breath. "I realize that's what we could do, Jessie. But making you my wife is what I want."

"No, it's not, Nate." She had hoped to hear him say those words for over two years, but she knew better than to believe he really wanted to get married. He'd broken up with her too many times for her to believe any such thing. "You might think that now. But we both know you'll lose interest within a few weeks and then you'd not only resent me and the baby for trapping you into doing something you didn't want to do, we'd be facing the heartbreak of a divorce."

"That's not going to happen, Jessie. When I make that commitment, it's for life." He ran his hand through his thick, straight hair. "I know I've let you down before, but—"

"Stop right there," she said, holding up her hand. "That's something else we need to get straight right here and now. I'm a big girl and I have no one else to blame but myself for allowing you to come and go in my life the way you've done. But the stakes are higher now, Nate. Disappointing me is one thing, but I refuse to allow you to upset our son or daughter. This is our child—my child—we're discussing and I swear I'll fight you with everything that's in me if you don't grow up and be there when he or she needs you. Being a parent isn't a game or something you run from whenever you get tired of playing the devoted daddy. It means you're there twenty-four/seven, no matter how tough it gets. If you can't handle that, then I'd rather you don't even bother."

"Jessie, I give you my word that from now on, you

and the baby are my top priority," he said, sounding sincere. He slid his hands from her shoulders down her arms to catch her hands in his. "I want us to get married and be a family. And I swear I will never cause you another minute of heartache."

"Then why did you make it sound as if you were going to be accepting responsibility for a crime instead of asking me to marry you?" she asked bluntly. "Did you even listen to yourself?"

"What do you mean?" he asked, looking bewildered.

"No woman wants to enter into a marriage with a man knowing that she was 'the right thing' for him to do," she said, shaking her head. "Besides, you had to take a deep breath before you could even get out that you want to make me your wife."

He stared at her for several long seconds before he finally spoke again. "Just give us a chance—give *me* a chance—darlin'. This is all new to me."

"Nate, I've already given you more chances than you deserve," she said, refusing to believe that this time would be any different than the others. He was only offering marriage because of the baby, not because he loved her and wanted them to build a life together.

"Do you have some vacation time you can take?" he asked suddenly.

"Yes, but I'm saving it for after the baby is born so that I can extend my maternity leave," she explained, wondering why he wanted to know.

"When is your next doctor's appointment?" he continued to question her.

"I have an ultrasound scheduled in two weeks," she answered. "Why are you asking about all of this?"

"I'd like for you to be here for the party tonight, then stay with me for the next couple of weeks," he said. He paused for a moment as if catching his breath. "Let me prove to you that getting married *is* what I want."

"I don't see how that's going to work," she pointed out. "You normally take a few more weeks than that to lose interest. Besides, you had to take a deep breath before you could tell me you wanted to prove how much you want us to get married. That doesn't instill a lot of confidence for the case you're trying to make. And all I'm hearing is what you want. Have you even considered what I want?"

He gave her a short nod before he asked, "What do you want, Jessie?"

"I want you to be a good father and love our child," she said slowly. "That's more important to me than anything else."

"I already love the baby and I give you my word that I'll be the best daddy I can possibly be."

She noticed that he failed to include her with his declaration. If she hadn't known before that the only reason he was offering marriage was because of the baby, she certainly did now.

"That's all I want from you," she said, when he continued to look at her expectantly.

"All I'm asking is to let me prove to you that being a good dad isn't the only thing I want. Stay with me until after Thanksgiving," he countered.

"Nate, I don't see how my staying here for a month

or even two weeks will prove anything," she said, shaking her head. He didn't love her and that was that. There was no sense wasting her vacation time on something that, in the end, wouldn't change that fact.

"What do you have to lose?" he asked.

"The vacation I intended to take after the baby is born," she answered. *As well as what's left of my heart after you broke it the last time.*

"If I can't convince you that I'm completely sincere about our being a family, then we'll call the lawyers and let them work out an agreement," he said, oblivious to her inner turmoil.

"I can't go to the party," she stalled. "I don't have anything to wear."

If she went along with his request and stayed for any length of time, she was afraid she would be tempted to fall back into their old pattern of him charming her into his bed. That was the last thing she wanted to happen. There was simply too much at stake now. The baby was counting on her to stay strong and resist the temptation Nate posed.

"I've already taken care of something for you to wear to the party," he said, looking quite pleased with himself. "I called Sam's wife, Bria. She and her sister, Mariah, were going to pick up their outfits at the costume shop up in Fort Worth. I asked her to pick out something for you and stop by one of the women's shops to get you a full change of clothes for tomorrow."

"Please tell me you didn't let her know about my pregnancy," she said, reaching up to rub at the sudden pounding in her temples.

"No, I thought we could tell everyone together to-night at the party," he said. "I just told Bria that you're about the size of our other sister-in-law Summer and that you liked your clothes nice and loose." He glanced down at her stomach. "I figured you might need a little extra room for the baby."

"I haven't said I would go to the party," she reminded him.

"You haven't said you wouldn't." His sexy grin told her he knew he was wearing her down.

She supposed that if she did stay, it would be as good a time as any to tell his family about the baby. And if she was present she would have a little more control over *what* he told them. As persistent as he was about convincing her to marry him, he'd probably tell his family that they were planning a trip down the aisle as well as about her pregnancy.

Being there to stop him from misleading his family would be the wisest choice. She wasn't going to marry him and set herself and the baby up for the heartbreak of watching him leave when he got bored.

"If I stay for the party, that doesn't mean I would be here for an extended period of time," she reminded him.

He stared at her for several long seconds before he cupped her face with his hands. "Jessie, you've experienced all of this from the moment you learned you were pregnant. But I've missed out on a lot these last four and a half months and I really don't want to miss any more. I promise that if you'll stay with me for the next month, I won't push for anything more than you're willing to give. This time will not only give us the opportunity to explore every option and be sure we're making the right decisions, it will give me the chance to feel like I'm really a part of this and get used to the idea of being a dad."

The sincerity in his voice and the heartfelt look on his face produced the results she was certain he had been going for. Now if she didn't stay, she'd feel so guilty about it she'd probably never be able to sleep again.

She'd had almost five months to get used to the idea of becoming a mother. Nate had had less than twenty-four hours to come to terms with being a father and she was sure it was still pretty unreal for him. And he did have a point about making decisions concerning how they raised their child. Their baby deserved to have its parents making the choices instead of stuffy lawyers spouting out legalese. She was going to have to figure out how to deal with Nate for the next eighteen or so years anyway. She might as well start now.

"I would have to go back home to get some clothes," she warned. Between now and the trip back to her apartment, she would hopefully be able to harden her resolve and shore up her defenses against his charismatic charm. In the past, she'd had about as much backbone as a jellyfish when it came to resisting Nate, and spending a month with him would be a true test of her willpower. But she could understand his wanting to take an active role in the pregnancy. It would be a good start to his bonding with the baby and that was something she wanted for her child.

"We can go to your place tomorrow and get whatever you need." His expression turned serious. "I really want this opportunity for us, Jessie. Please say you'll stay."

She might have had a chance if he had been demanding or insistent. But the sincere tone of his voice and the hopeful look in his eyes were impossible to resist. Maybe she needed this test to prove to herself that they could raise their child together without her falling into bed with him again.

"All right, I'll arrange to take the time off and stay until the weekend after Thanksgiving," she heard herself say. "But only on one condition."

"What's that, darlin'?" he asked, lowering his head to brush her lips with his.

"I don't want any pressure from you about getting married," she stated flatly as she backed away from him.

"I promise."

"I'm only here for you to prove to me that you're sincere about wanting this baby as much as I do and to work out custody and visitation." As an afterthought, she added, "And just for the record, at night I'll be staying in one room and you'll be staying in another."

Two

Standing with his brothers at the makeshift bar his hired men had constructed for the party, Nate was only half listening to the conversation about his brother's rodeo stock company and the bucking bulls he owned that had been selected for the National Finals Rodeo. He was too busy watching Jessie. She was as cute as a button in the girl garden-gnome costume that Bria had picked up for her to wear to the party. She'd had to leave the vest off because it was too formfitting, but the white apron over her full red skirt hid her rounded stomach just fine.

Seated on a bale of hay, Jessie was listening attentively to his two nephews Seth and little Hank jabber about their new ponies. He could tell by the way she smiled at the little boys going on about riding their "horsies" that she loved kids. When his niece Katie toddled over to her, Jessie picked up the baby girl to sit on her lap without a moment's hesitation. She was going to be a great mom, and he could only hope to be half as good of a dad.

His heart stuttered and he had to take a deep breath to chase away the fear tightening his chest. Just the thought of being a daddy scared the living spit out of him. What if he couldn't live up to the responsibility? He was a fantastic uncle to his niece and nephews. But that role didn't carry nearly as much responsibility as being a father. What kind of dad would he be?

His biggest fear had always been that he would turn out to be as negligent and undependable as his and Sam's father had been. That's why he'd never really thought about having kids. Hell, he hadn't even thought about having a wife because of it. But it was all he'd been able to think about for the past twenty-four hours. Could he live up to his responsibilities?

Of the six men he called his brothers, Sam was his only biological sibling and had turned out to be as solid as a rock. He was the exact opposite of their old man, and it gave Nate hope that he would be just as reliable as Sam. But how would he know for sure?

"So what's up with you, Nate?" T. J. Malloy asked, interrupting Nate's disturbing thoughts.

"Yeah, this is the first time you've asked the little blond to join one of our family get-togethers," Ryder McClain added, grinning from ear to ear.

"Maybe now that he owns the Twin Oaks Ranch, Nate is finally ready to settle down," Lane Donaldson speculated as he cradled his infant son in the crook of his arm.

"I've got a hundred bucks that says he and Jessie are married by spring," Sam said, glancing from Nate to Jessie and back. "Yesterday when she called to ask me where she could find you, she sounded pretty determined."

"Jessie called you and you didn't tell me?" Nate demanded, glaring at his older brother.

Sam shrugged. "She asked me not to and I told her I wouldn't. And you know as well as the rest of us about Hank's number-one rule."

"Yeah," Nate said, his irritation fading at the mention of their foster father and the personal code of ethics he had taught the boys in his care. "Break a bone if you have to before you break your word."

His brothers all nodded in agreement.

Jaron Lambert pulled his wallet from the hip pocket of his jeans, got out a hundred-dollar bill and plunked it down on the top of the bar. "I say Nate and Jessie will be hitched by the middle of this coming summer."

"I've got Christmas," T.J. said, adding his money to the pool.

"I'll take Valentine's Day," Lane spoke up, putting his hundred with the rest.

Ryder pulled his wallet from the hip pocket of his jeans, then looked him up and down before he slapped Nate on the shoulder. "I'm betting they'll be married by Thanksgiving."

Nate shook his head as he listened to his brothers bet on when he and Jessie took a trip down the aisle. It had always been this way with the brothers. From the time they were all placed into the care of their foster father, Hank Calvert on the Last Chance Ranch, the six of them had a betting pool going on just about everything. Of course back then they had all been dirt poor and had nothing better to do than speculate on the next time it rained or which one of them would be the first to win a buckle at one of the junior rodeos they all competed in.

Now that they were all self-made millionaires, instead of betting fifty cents or a dollar, the stakes were a lot higher. These days it was nothing for them to bet a hundred dollars or more on who would be the next one to tie the knot or add to the family with the birth of a baby. But up until yesterday, he hadn't even considered the possibility that he would be the next one they speculated on or that they would all be right in doing so.

Every time one of them mentioned him getting hitched he felt a twitch at the corner of his left eye. He still couldn't believe that he was finally willing to take the plunge and get married. It scared the living hell out of him that he might let Jessie and their baby down. But he had a responsibility to both of them and he was going to do everything in his power to live up to what a good husband and father should be.

Focusing on the pile of money on the bar to keep himself from dwelling on all of the what-ifs, Nate shook his head. "While you all waste your time and money, I'm going to ask Jessie to dance." The kids had abandoned her in favor of playing with a cardboard box someone had left over by the refreshment table, and he decided now might be a good time to find out when she wanted to tell his family about the baby.

He threw his empty beer bottle in the recycling bin at the end of the bar and walked away. He was in enough trouble with her. He didn't want to add more by telling the guys about her pregnancy before she was ready. And if he stuck around much longer, there was a real possibility of him accidently tipping them off that something was up. If that happened, they would needle him until hell froze over trying to get him to tell them what was going on.

Hiding things from the people who knew you best wasn't all that easy. That was the only downside he could see about being so close and knowing each other so well. But he wouldn't have it any other way. He knew he could count on his brothers being there for him no matter what, just as he would be there for them.

"Are you having a good time, darlin'?" he asked, walking up to where Jessie still sat on the bale of straw.

With her attention on the kids, she smiled. "I'm having a wonderful time. But I'm apparently not nearly as interesting as a cardboard box."

Nate took her hands in his to pull her to her feet. "Just wait until you see the kids at Christmas. They get all kinds of excited and can't wait for us to remove the toys from the boxes. Then they toss the toy aside and sit down to play with the box."

Her light laughter made his insides vibrate with a tension he knew all too well. He wanted her. Hell, even during the times when he'd broken things off with her and gone his own way, he'd still wanted her. Maybe that was the reason he hadn't been able to stay away from her. He had a feeling the reasons went much deeper, but he wasn't going to think about that now. He wanted to hold her in his arms without having her remind him that she wasn't there to rekindle their romance.

"Would you like to dance, darlin'?" She loved kicking up her heels on the dance floor and he wanted her to enjoy herself. If she had a good time, it might remind her of what they had shared in the past.

"I think I would, sheriff," she said, referring to the tin badge he had pinned to his shirt.

He nodded to the frontman in the band he'd hired and, right on cue, they ended the song they had been playing and immediately launched into a popular slow country song. When the group had first arrived, he'd told the man the title of the song he wanted them to play and to be watching for his signal. It was the song he and Jessie had danced to the first time he'd taken her out for a night on the town.

"You had that planned," she accused.

Grinning, he took her into his arms and swept her out onto the dance floor. "Yup." He leaned close to whisper in her ear. "You didn't tell me I wasn't allowed to remind you of the first date we went on or how good we are together." He wisely refrained from mentioning that was true for other things besides dancing.

He felt her tremble against him a moment before she put a little space between them. "Nate, the first thing we're going to do after this party is to set down some ground rules. Otherwise, I'll be going home tomorrow and I won't be back."

"Sure thing, darlin'," he said agreeably as they swayed in time with the music.

She could lay down all the rules she wanted, but that little shiver was all the indication he needed to know that she wasn't impervious to him. And he had every intention of reminding her of that fact every chance he got.

He waited until the song ended before he asked, "When do you want to make the announcement about the baby?"

She sighed. "I suppose now is as good of a time as any. But don't you dare mislead your family into believing that we're getting married because we're not."

"I give you my word," he said, nodding. He wasn't about to do anything that would send her running back to Waco before the end of the month they had agreed on. And that was exactly what would happen if he so much as hinted to his family that marriage was a possibility. Besides, he had until just after Thanksgiving to figure out how he was going to accomplish that goal. He was determined not to fail. He wanted her to agree to be his wife and for them to be married before the baby was born.

Putting his arm around her shoulders to guide her, they walked over to Bria and her sister, Mariah, chatting with some of their friends by the refreshment table. "Bria, could you get the family together and meet Jessie and I outside for a few minutes? We have something we'd like to tell everyone."

"Of course, Nate." Smiling, his sister-in-law turned

to Mariah. "Go tell the men to meet us outside while I find Summer, Taylor and Heather."

Within a few minutes Nate and Jessie stood just outside of the big barn doors, surrounded by his family. He knew his sisters-in-law would be excited by their news and would start making plans for baby showers and whatever else women did to welcome a new baby into the family. But his brothers were going to give him hell when they learned that marriage wasn't a sure thing.

Their foster father had raised them with a clear sense of what was right and wrong. From the time they had been old enough to start dating, Hank Calvert had told them it was their responsibility to protect a woman. And in the case of an accidental pregnancy, a man had a moral obligation to do what was right and give the woman and child his name.

Nate knew that in this day and time, that way of thinking might be considered antiquated, but there was no man he respected more than his late foster father. Hank's teachings had served him and his brothers well over the years and turned them from rebellious young hell-raisers into honest, upstanding adults. As far as he was concerned, that kind of guidance shouldn't be ignored. Besides, the thought of having Jessie at his side every day and in his bed every night was a very appealing aspect of marriage, even if it did scare the hell out of him.

"So what's up, bro?" Jaron asked with one of his rare smiles. The quiet, brooding one of his brothers, Jaron was the only one that Nate knew for certain hadn't completely rid himself of the ghosts of his past. They all had had a few residual hang-ups from their lives before being sent to the Last Chance Ranch. But Jaron's ran deeper than the rest of them.

"Yeah, spill the beans, hotshot," T.J. chimed in.

Nate glanced at Jessie as he reached for her hand. "We just wanted to let you know that we'll be adding another member to the family in a few months. We're going to have a baby."

There was a stunned silence that followed his announcement and one look at the expression on Sam's face let Nate know his failure to mention a wedding had not gone unnoticed. With a slight shake of his head, he let his brothers know not to ask about it until later. He knew they would respect his wishes and remain silent—for now. But as soon as the opportunity presented itself, he was going to have some explaining to do.

"That's wonderful," Bria said, breaking the silence as she stepped forward to hug him and Jessie. God bless her, Bria could read a situation faster than anyone he knew and always seemed to know exactly what to say to ease the tension.

"I'm so excited for you," Summer McClain added happily, shifting her daughter to her hip in order to reach out and hug Jessie.

"We've got another baby shower to plan," Lane's wife, Taylor, spoke up enthusiastically. "I've got some new appetizers in mind that will be perfect for the refreshments." A personal chef, Taylor was always looking for reasons to try new recipes on the family.

"When is the baby due?" T.J.'s wife, Heather, asked.

"In late March or early April," Jessie answered. Nate

could tell by the tone in her voice she was relieved that no one had asked about a wedding.

"Do you know if you're having a boy or a girl?" Mariah asked, giving Jaron a pointed look. Every time one of the sisters-in-law became pregnant, Mariah and Jaron argued about what gender they thought the baby would be. It appeared this time was going to be no different.

Jessie smiled as she shook her head. "I'm having an ultrasound in a couple of weeks to find out."

"Congratulations," Sam finally said, stepping forward to give Jessie a brotherly hug. He stared hard at Nate. "I think this calls for a beer, don't you?"

"Great news," Ryder said, wrapping Jessie in a bear hug. When he put his hand on Nate's shoulder, Nate could tell by Ryder's iron grip that he was about to be escorted to the bar for his brothers' interrogation.

"Jessie, if you don't mind, we'd like to take this bonehead back to the bar to toast your good news," Lane explained, handing his baby son over to his wife, Taylor.

"I don't mind," she said, smiling. "It will give me a chance to ask your wives what I can expect with a newborn and what baby products they've found to be the most useful."

As his brothers walked him back into the barn, Nate heard the excited voices of the women as they offered their suggestions on what they thought Jessie might need to get ready for the baby. He wasn't the least bit surprised. Whether she realized it or not, she and the baby were already considered members of his family and everyone would do whatever they could to help her and make her feel welcome.

"Okay, what's the story, bro?" Sam demanded when they reached the bar.

"And why didn't we hear that the two of you are making plans to get hitched?" T.J. asked as he motioned for the bartender to get them all a bottle of beer.

"You all know about as much as I do," Nate admitted as they walked over to a more private area away from a group of their friends. "Jessie showed up yesterday to tell me she's about four and a half months pregnant, I'm the daddy and when I told her we'd get married as soon as possible, she flat-out refused."

"You *told* her you'd marry her instead of asking her to be your wife?" Lane asked, his expression incredulous.

"Way to sweet-talk a woman, bro," Jaron said, shaking his head. "Even I know better than to do that."

"For a ladies' man, you sure screwed that up," Ryder stated disgustedly.

"And you tried to give me advice on how to talk to a woman when Heather and I first started seeing each other." T.J. took a swig of beer from the bottle in his hand. "I'm glad I had the good sense not to listen to you."

Sam folded his arms across his chest and glared at him. "How do you intend to straighten this out with her, Nate?"

"I've already come up with a plan," he answered, watching the women and kids reenter the barn. They all looked as if they were having a lot better time than he was at the moment.

"You want to run this scheme of yours past us and get our input before you try to execute it?" Lane asked.

"Yeah, the way you messed up that proposal, it sounds to me like you need all the help you can get," Jaron added.

As much as he had riding on the outcome, Nate figured he could use some advice from his brothers and especially from Lane. Having the opinion of a licensed psychologist definitely couldn't hurt and might just give him the edge he needed to convince Jessie of his sincerity.

"I got her to agree to stay with me until after Thanksgiving so we can work out joint custody and how we're going to raise the baby," Nate answered. He stared across the dance floor at Jessie and the rest of the women. "And while I'm at it, I'm going to pull out all the stops and show her that I really do want to get married."

"The way things have gone down with you two in the past, you've got your work cut out for you." T.J. stated what Nate was certain all of his brothers were thinking.

"It for damned sure isn't going to be easy," Ryder added.

"And there's no margin for error," Lane warned. "If you don't get it right this time, they'll be passing out ice water in hell before you get a second chance."

Nate nodded. No matter how scary it was to commit himself to one woman, especially knowing that he'd have to reveal everything about his past, he had too much to lose not to do everything in his power to make things right between them. "I'm going to get Jessie to agree to marry me or die trying."

As Jessie listened to Nate's sisters-in-law discuss possible themes for the baby shower they were planning for her and the refreshments they might serve, she couldn't help but feel envious of the strong family bond the women and their husbands shared. Over the past couple of years, Nate had told her a little about his blended family, and how he and Sam met the other four men they called brothers when they were placed in the foster care system.

Sent to the Last Chance Ranch as teenagers, the six boys had found their salvation as well as each other, thanks to a kindhearted man named Hank Calvert and his unique set of rules to live by. The boys he fostered had stayed tight throughout the ensuing years and from what she could see, the women they married had become just as close.

"When you find out the baby's gender do you intend to tell everyone or let it be a surprise?" Heather asked.

"I thought I'd let everyone know the gender, but keep the name secret until the baby is born," Jessie said, resting her hand on her stomach. "I know it sounds strange, but I'd like to introduce him or her to everyone by name."

"If you don't mind, could you let us know what you're having as soon as you have the ultrasound, Jessie?"

Summer asked, smiling. "That way we'll know what colors to use for decorations."

"And if you've chosen the colors for the nursery, that might be useful as well," Heather added as her little boy, Seth, ran up to hand her a bouquet of dried weeds he'd obviously picked out of a hay bale. After she thanked him and gave him a kiss, he rejoined the other two toddlers. "T.J. gave me a bouquet of flowers the other day and Seth tries to mimic everything his daddy does."

"That's so sweet." Jessie found the little boy's gesture very touching and she knew for certain she would be just as happy having a boy as she would having a girl.

"It would also be helpful if you register at one of the baby boutiques in Waco as soon as you can so we can put that on the invitations," Bria suggested, bringing the conversation back to the shower they were planning.

"They're using some of the most unusual combinations of colors these days," Taylor commented as she shifted her baby son to her shoulder for a burp after he finished the bottle she had been giving him. "I hadn't even considered the colors I used until I saw them in one of the baby boutiques."

"I hope you get to decorate with a lot of pink and purple for a little princess," Mariah stated as she got up from the bale of straw she was sitting on to walk over to the three toddlers playing with the box again.

"That's only because she wants another excuse to argue with Jaron," Taylor confided. She got up and picked up a diaper bag. "Time to get this little man changed and settled down for the night."

As Taylor walked out of the barn toward the house to get her son ready for bed, Bria explained the ongoing disagreement between Mariah and Jaron. "Whenever one of us announces that a new baby will be joining the family, Mariah insists it will be a girl and Jaron is just as determined it will be a boy." Shaking her head, she sighed. "It's their way of dancing around the real issue between them."

Jessie nodded. "Nate mentioned that Jaron and your sister have been attracted to each other for years, but he thinks he's too old for her."

"When she was eighteen, a nine-year gap in their ages did make a difference in maturity and experience," Bria said. "But now that she's twenty-five and he's thirty-four, Jaron is the only one who thinks it still matters."

"I'm twenty-six and Nate's thirty-three. Neither of us have given the seven-year age difference a second thought. I wonder why he's so insistent that it's a problem?" Jessie asked, frowning.

"If you can answer that, you will have solved one of the mysteries of the universe," Summer stated as she hurried over to keep her daughter from trying to stand on a pumpkin.

An hour later as she helped the women clear the refreshment table, Jessie was more envious than ever of the love and devotion they all shared. They might be a blended family, but they were closer than some people she'd seen who were related by blood.

She sighed heavily as she thought about her own family. For whatever reason, her parents had never seemed to care if she and her older brother had a close relationship. Of course, her brother had been a junior in high school when she was born and as with most teenage boys, he thought he had better things to do than to pay attention to his baby sister.

Unfortunately, she wasn't really all that close to her parents either. Her mother and father were real estate brokers and when they weren't busy selling mansions to the überrich residents of Houston, they were attending a social function at the country club to make more contacts for their agency. About the only time she could remember them paying all that much attention to her was when she told them she was going to become a registered nurse instead of earning a business degree in college. They had both been extremely disappointed with her decision and couldn't understand why she didn't want to follow in their footsteps like her brother had done.

That hadn't changed since she graduated and started her career. Sadly, she didn't hold out a lot of hope they would react any differently when she finally told them about the baby either. They were simply too caught up in brokering real estate deals to be bothered with family. And the only reason they had more to do with her brother was because he was just as driven by the almighty dollar as they were and had joined the family business.

"Do you have plans for Thanksgiving, Jessie?" Bria

asked, bringing her back to the present. "If not, we'd love to have you spend the day with us."

"I usually work most of the holidays," Jessie answered, omitting the fact that she volunteered for those days. Spending time at the hospital was preferable to the periods of awkward silence that always seemed to develop whenever she visited her parents. "Could I let you know a bit later?"

"Of course," Bria said. Her voice barely above a whisper, she added, "I'm sure you and Nate have a lot of things you need to work out. But I want you to know that whatever happens, you and the baby are always welcome anytime we have a get-together."

Touched by the gesture, Jessie blinked away tears. "Thank you. That means a lot."

Several minutes later, Nate's brothers and their wives hugged Jessie and told her how happy they were that she'd joined them for the evening and how thrilled they were about the baby. As she watched them depart, she had to fight the wistfulness building inside her. She had always longed to be part of a family like Nate's—to have that kind of unconditional support and acceptance.

But as tempting as it was, she couldn't allow the lure of a close, loving family to influence her decision when it came to Nate's offer of marriage. When she made that commitment, she refused to settle for anything less than love from her husband. However, it gave her immeasurable comfort knowing her baby was already anticipated and welcomed into such a wonderful family.

"Did you have a good time, darlin'?" Nate asked as they started walking toward the house.

Jessie nodded. "It was good to see your brothers and Bria again. I hadn't seen them since Sam was in the hospital a few years ago. And I'm glad I got to meet your other sisters-in-law and Mariah. They're all very nice."

"My brothers can be real pains in the ass sometimes," he said, giving her a grin that never failed to take her breath away. "But I wouldn't trade them for anything. They have my back and I have theirs. And their wives are real sweethearts. They all go out of their way to make sure the family stays close by having dinners and throwing parties like we had tonight."

As they entered the house, she did her best to ignore Nate's charming expression and focus on the fact that he hadn't invited her to any of his family gatherings in the past. She had a feeling she knew why. It had been his attempt to keep their relationship casual and to discourage her from thinking that what they had between them was more serious. But as much as that fact bothered her, she couldn't really hold his reluctance for her to be around his family against him.

She *had* avoided introducing him to her family as well. While he'd been determined to keep things light, she had been trying to spare him a cold reception and an uncomfortable interrogation about the size of his net worth. But he hadn't seemed to notice that she hadn't introduced him to her parents and she wasn't going to call attention to it.

"Is something wrong?" he asked when they started up the stairs.

Startled out of her musing by his question, she shook her head. "No. I'm just a bit tired." She wasn't about to tell him the real reason behind her pensive mood. That was something two people who were in a relationship would share and she wasn't about to go there. That might give him the idea she was getting closer to resuming their relationship, which she wasn't.

When they walked down the hall and stopped in front of her bedroom door, he didn't try to put his arms around her as she thought he might. Instead, he smiled as he cupped her cheek with his palm. "I'll be right back," he said, crossing the hall to disappear into the master suite. When he returned, he handed her a white T-shirt. "Since I failed to have Bria pick up something for you to sleep in, I thought this would be more comfortable than sleeping in your clothes."

"Thank you," she said, accepting the garment. Until he mentioned it, she hadn't given what she would sleep in a second thought.

"I'm glad you had a good time. Sleep well, darlin'." Leaning forward, he kissed her forehead, then reaching around her, opened the bedroom door for her to enter. "I'll see you in the morning."

Staring up into his blue eyes, she swallowed hard. Why was she disappointed that Nate hadn't really kissed her? This was the way she wanted it to be between them.

"Good night, Nate," she said, escaping into the room and closing the door firmly behind her.

What was wrong with her? She didn't want *that* kind of attention from Nate Rafferty. He'd proven that she couldn't put her faith and trust in him not to hurt her. She had done so over and over, and each time he'd left her to pick up the pieces of her broken heart.

Now that they were having a baby and their lives would always be tied together, it was even more important to protect herself from heartbreak. It would be so much easier raising the baby if they could at least be friends.

Sighing, Jessie took off the gnome costume and slipped into the T-shirt Nate had given her to sleep in. She was immediately assailed by Nate's clean masculine scent and a shiver of longing slid up her spine. Chiding herself for her reaction, she climbed into bed and it crossed her mind that when she went back home tomorrow, it would definitely be in her best interest to stay there. But she had told Nate she would stay with him until after Thanksgiving so they could make decisions and to give him a chance to feel as if he was a part of the pregnancy.

Jessie turned to her side and tried to stop thinking about how he had originally asked her to stay in order to convince her he wanted to get married. She had no doubt that Nate had convinced himself that was what he wanted. But she wasn't foolish enough to think he could change his mind that fast about something he wouldn't even consider a remote possibility until she announced she was pregnant.

He'd only suggested it because of the baby. It had nothing to do with loving her. As far as she was concerned, love was the only reason a couple should consider entering into a marriage.

She closed her eyes tight against her threatening tears. She had stopped wondering why Nate couldn't love her and resigned herself to the fact that he never would. But that didn't stop her from remembering how gently he touched her or from longing for the safety she always felt when she was wrapped securely in his strong arms.

Three

Late the following afternoon, after driving to Waco to get Jessie's clothes and stopping by the hospital for her to make arrangements to take off work for the next month, Nate couldn't help but smile as he carried Jessie's luggage into the ranch house and up the stairs to the room across from the master suite. How could one petite woman need so many clothes? He'd carried in two large suitcases that were so stuffed he was surprised the zippers hadn't given way, a smaller one that was just as full and a good-sized tote bag. And all the way back to Twin Oaks she'd worried that she might have forgotten something. He chuckled. As long as he had access to a washer and dryer, he could get by indefinitely with whatever he could fit into a gym bag and a boot carrier for his dress boots.

While Jessie went to work hanging things in the closet and filling dresser drawers, Nate looked around the room. "You know, this bedroom would be the obvious choice to turn into a nursery."

"Why would you need a nursery?" she asked, stopping to look at him. "You won't be having the baby overnight until he or she is older."

"And why won't I?" He shook his head. "When I told you I wanted to be part of the baby's life, I meant starting from the day he's born."

She took a deep breath and finished putting several pairs of socks into the dresser drawer before she turned to face him. "While I'm glad to hear you want to be a hands-on dad, you having the baby by yourself for more than a few hours won't be possible."

"Why not?" he asked, folding his arms across his chest. "Don't you think I can handle it?"

"Not unless you grow a pair of breasts and start producing milk," she shot back, laughing.

"Oh," he said, rubbing the back of his neck with his hand. "I, uh, hadn't thought about that."

Her smile was indulgent when she walked over to place her hand on his arm. "I'm not saying you won't be part of the baby's life while he or she is an infant. I'm just trying to tell you that for a few months it would be impractical for you to have the baby for any length of time."

The feel of her hand on his arm through his chambray shirt sent a shaft of longing from the top of his head to the soles of his feet. It had been months since he'd lost himself in her softness and the slight widening of her pretty violet eyes was a good indication that he wasn't the only one remembering that fact. It was all he could do to keep from reaching for her. But he'd given his word he wouldn't push things.

Forcing himself to concentrate on what she'd said, he had to admit Jessie had a valid point. But he wasn't going to give up that easily.

"Then how are you going to handle going back to work if you breast-feed?" he asked, frowning.

"With maternity leave and the vacation days that I've saved, I'll be off until the baby is three or four months old," she answered. "I'm sure I'll be able to work something out after that."

He covered her hand with his. "It looks like that's the first issue we need to put on the list of things we'll have to work out."

"I suppose so," she murmured, slipping her hand from beneath his and turning back to the bag she had been unpacking.

As he stood there wishing he could take her in his arms, Nate did his best to shore up his patience. He had told his brothers he would pull out all the stops to get her to marry him. But he had to take his time if he had any chance of convincing her that he really wanted to make her his wife. Rushing her would only send Jessie running back to Waco faster than a New York minute.

"After you get your things put away, I thought we'd drive over to Beaver Dam for supper at the Broken Spoke," he said, deciding it was time to put his plan into action. "Today is my housekeeper's day off and I'll be the first to admit I'm not much of a cook."

"I could make something for us if you'd rather stay in this evening," she offered, reaching into the tote bag to remove what looked to be some kind of wedge-shaped pillow.

Nate briefly wondered what it was, but just as quickly dismissed it as he shook his head. "The day's been pretty busy already and I'm sure you're more than ready to relax and enjoy the rest of the evening."

He purposely omitted that the Broken Spoke Bar and Grill had a nice little dance floor and a jukebox filled with slow country love songs. Many a cowboy had used that dance floor and songs on that old juke-box as an excuse to hold his woman close while they swayed in time to the music. Nate fully intended to continue the tradition with Jessie.

"All right," she finally said, emptying the last suit-case. She glanced down at the clothes she had on. "Will what I'm wearing be appropriate or should I change into something less casual?"

"The food is pretty good, but the Broken Spoke isn't fancy." He glanced at her jeans and loose mint-green shirt. "What you're wearing is just fine."

"Then I guess I'm ready whenever you are," she said, picking up her shoulder bag.

As he stepped back for her to precede him from the room, Nate swallowed hard. He hadn't really paid a lot of attention to the size of Jessie's belly until now. But her gauzy shirt highlighted the small bulge more than concealed it, unlike her sweatshirt and the gnome costume's apron had done the day before.

He took a deep breath as they left the house and he

helped her into the passenger side of his truck. He had never given much thought to a pregnant woman's figure and the effect it had on her sex appeal. But there was no other way to describe Jessie other than sexy as hell. Even though she wore loose clothing, he could tell that her breasts were larger and her smooth complexion seemed to have a glow about it that begged for his touch. And for reasons he didn't even want to think about, just the thought that she was carrying his child made him want her.

Shaking his head, he rounded the front of the truck and climbed in behind the steering wheel. Had he lost his mind? He'd never in his entire life given a pregnant woman, and whether or not she was attractive, a second thought.

As he started the truck and steered it down the lane to the main road, Nate decided not to think too much about the reasons behind his finding Jessie so alluring. He had always desired her and that was something that would never change. Of course, he would feel different about her now than other women. She was the mother of his child. The woman he was going to make his wife, even if he wasn't sure he could live up to expectations.

When a knot formed in the pit of his stomach and his palms started to sweat, he tried to focus on something—anything else. Even if he didn't know how to go about it, he was going to give it everything he had in him, and be the best husband and father he could possibly be.

Jessie looked around when she and Nate entered the Broken Spoke Bar and Grill. It was typical of a lot of small-town Texas watering holes in big ranch country. The red vinyl seats on the chrome chairs and booths had a few repaired cracks and the Formica tabletops had seen so much use they had faded from shiny to a dull, flat black. But as dated and well used as the decor was, everything appeared to be neat and clean.

"Will this be all right?" Nate asked as he guided her to a table toward the back of the room.

"It's fine," she said as she continued to look around.

Several men dressed in worn jeans, work shirts and denim jackets sat on stools at the bar talking to a couple of women, while a few others played pool. They all wore wide-brimmed hats and scuffed boots, indicating they most likely worked on some of the many ranches in the area.

"There aren't very many women," Jessie commented when Nate held her chair for her.

He shrugged and lowered himself into the chair beside her. "There are quite a few more on Friday and Saturday nights, but even then the men outnumber the women."

"What can I get for you folks this evenin'?" a young ponytailed waitress asked, walking up to the table.

Jessie looked at Nate. "What are you having?"

"My usual," he said, grinning. "Steak, home fries, coleslaw and a beer."

"I'll have the same," she decided. "But instead of the beer, I'd like a glass of milk, please."

"You got it." Nodding, the waitress snapped her chewing gum as she wrote down their orders. "How do y'all want those steaks cooked?"

After telling the girl how they liked their steaks, they made small talk for a few minutes before Nate reached over to cover Jessie's hand with his. "Jessie, I think I've come up with a way that we can both be with the baby during his first year."

"Or her first year," she corrected as she removed her hand from beneath his. His calloused palm on her skin was a distraction she didn't need. "The baby might be a girl."

His smile when he nodded made her feel warm all over. "Either way, I don't want to miss out on all the things that other dads get to experience. That's why I think you should move to the ranch."

She could understand and was even encouraged by his desire to be part of their baby's most formative year, but she wasn't going to marry him. "Nate, I told you I don't want to be pressured. I'm not going to do something that we both know would end in disaster."

"Hear me out, darlin'," he said, his expression turning serious. "I'm not going to lie to you. I do want us to get married and I'm not going to give up on that. But that isn't what I'm talking about right now. I'm suggesting that you move to the ranch and let me be part of the rest of your pregnancy as well as the baby's first year."

Before she could answer, the waitress brought their dinner and Jessie waited until the girl walked over to another table before she commented on his outrageous proposal. "I can understand you wanting to be there to see all of the baby's firsts, but I can't move to your ranch, Nate. My job is in Waco."

"You can take a leave of absence," he said as if it

would be the easiest thing in the world to do. He picked up his knife and fork to cut into his steak. "Or if you want to continue working, you could get a job at the hospital or one of the doctor's offices around Stephenville. It's not nearly as big as the hospital where you work in Waco, but small hospitals have sick people, too."

"I realize that. But why would I want to trade a five-minute commute for a half-hour drive?" she asked, sitting back from the table to stare at him. "You could always move to Waco."

He shrugged. "I have a lot more room at Twin Oaks than you have in your apartment. Besides, there's one big advantage if you moved to the ranch."

"And what would that be?" she asked, picking up her fork to spear one of the potato wedges on her plate.

"You would have help with the baby and wouldn't have to worry about finding someone to babysit while you're working," he said, reaching for his beer.

"That would be great during the week, but what about the weekends? You're normally competing in a rodeo somewhere out of state and even if it's here in Texas, it would require that you find a place to stay for a night or two." She shook her head. "The chances of me having weekends off if I worked at a hospital are extremely slim. Who would keep the baby then?"

"I'm pretty sure we can work it out," he said, smiling. "But we've got plenty of time. It's just one option to consider."

They fell silent while they ate and by the time they finished, Jessie had pushed his suggestion to the back of her mind. He might think it was a viable solution, but she knew better. It was going to be a true test of her willpower living at the ranch for a month. There was no way she could be with him for over a year without falling victim to his charismatic charm again.

"I think I'll check out what songs they have on the jukebox," Nate said, rising from the table.

As she watched him walk across the small dance area, Jessie caught her lower lip between her teeth. Nate's shoulders were impressively wide and filled out his chambray shirt to perfection. A shiver of longing slid up her spine when she thought about how it felt to be surrounded by all that masculinity as he made love to her.

If just watching him caused that kind of reaction, she was in serious trouble. How on earth was she going to resist his allure for the next month?

Lost in thought, she jumped when Nate walked up beside her and reached down to take her hand in his. "I think that's our song, darlin'. Would you like to dance?"

Before she could protest, he pulled her to her feet and ushered her out onto the dance floor. "Nate, this isn't a good idea."

"Why? Are you too tired?" he asked, wrapping his arms around her.

"N-no." It hadn't even occurred to her to use the excuse he'd handed her.

"It's just a dance, Jessie," he whispered close to her ear.

With his body aligned fully with hers and his warm breath feathering over her sensitive skin, she couldn't remember her own name, let alone come up with a good reason why they shouldn't be dancing. But as his body moved against hers, Jessie gave in to the impulse to lean closer and the longing that rushed through her body was almost overwhelming.

As Nate moved them in time to the music, the feel of his rapidly hardening body sent a wave of heat coursing from the top of her head to the soles of her feet. Her knees wobbled and she had no choice but to cling to him to keep from melting into a puddle at his big, booted feet.

When the song ended, she drew on every ounce of strength she had left and pulled from his arms. "I—I must be more tired than I thought," she lied as she faked a yawn. "We should probably leave."

He stared down at her for a moment before he grinned. "Whatever you say, darlin'."

They both knew she was fibbing, but to her relief, Nate didn't call her on the ruse and after tossing money on the table for their dinner along with a generous tip, he placed his hand to the small of her back to guide her to the exit. Neither spoke as he helped her up into the truck and the ride back to his ranch was just as silent.

"Would you like to watch a movie?" he asked, when he parked the truck between his Mercedes sports car and her SUV in the three-car garage. He got out of the truck and came around to open the passenger door for her. "I noticed the newest Melissa McCarthy comedy is on pay-per-view."

He knew the actress was one of her favorites and she was tempted, but on the ride home she realized that she really was tired. "Could we take a rain check on that? There's a good chance I would fall asleep in the middle of it."

"Sure," he said, lifting her down from the truck seat. "We can watch it tomorrow night and I'll get Rosemary to make us some popcorn." As they walked into the house, he asked, "Or would you prefer to drive up to Stephenville for dinner and a movie?"

Although going out was tempting, it sounded too much like a date. That wasn't what she was there for and she certainly didn't want to give Nate the false impression that she was falling under his spell yet again.

"Staying here for a movie is fine with me," she answered decisively as they climbed the stairs. "I'll be able to turn in right after it's over."

When they reached her room, he stopped her when she started to open the door. "Do you think you'll feel up to going with me to the rodeo up in Amarillo this coming weekend?" he asked.

"Why wouldn't I?" she asked, frowning. "I'm not ill, I'm pregnant."

"I wasn't sure if you thought it would be too tiring," he said, reaching up to rub the back of his neck with his hand. "I'll be the first to admit that I don't know all that much about how a pregnant woman feels or what she should or shouldn't do."

Unable to stop herself, she placed her hand on his arm. "Other than becoming seriously addicted to naps, I feel good," she said, smiling. "So good in fact, I plan on working right up until the baby is born."

"Okay. Let me go back and rephrase my question. Would you go with me to the rodeo this weekend?"

She knew she should tell him no and be content with a little alone time so that she could think. But she just couldn't resist the chance to finally see how good of a rodeo rider he was. In the two and a half years they'd known each other, Nate had never asked her to watch him compete, and she wasn't about to miss the opportunity. Between her work schedule and the fact that she was on duty most weekends, it had made sense. But it would have been nice if he had at least asked her to go with him when they'd been seeing each other, even if she would have had to turn him down.

"I'd like that." Knowing they would need to be there for two or three nights, she felt compelled to add, "As long as we have separate rooms."

"Of course." Tracing his index finger along her jaw, he leaned forward to kiss her forehead. "Sweet dreams, darlin'."

The feel of his lips on her skin and the look of longing in his eyes stole her breath and it took everything she had in her to turn, walk into the bedroom and shut the door. Releasing the breath she'd been holding, Jessie changed into her nightshirt and grabbed her wedge pillow before climbing into bed. Once she'd turned to her side and arranged the pillow to support her stomach and one of the bed pillows to support her back, she found herself staring at the closed door, wondering if Nate was going to have as much trouble going to sleep as she knew she would.

As a deep sadness began to fill her, a lone tear trickled down her cheek. She impatiently swiped it away with the back of her hand. What was wrong with her? Why did she feel such a keen sense of disappointment?

He was doing exactly as she had asked him to do. Although he had admitted over dinner that he hadn't given up on wanting them to get married, he wasn't pressing the issue. And other than a couple of chaste kisses to the forehead and holding her when they danced, he hadn't made a move toward a more intimate caress.

The baby chose that moment to move and placing her hand on her stomach, Jessie bit her lip as she tried to fight the wave of emotion threatening to swamp her. She missed Nate holding her, loving her. In all of her twenty-six years, she'd never felt as safe and secure as when she was in his arms. But she couldn't let her emotions sway her.

This was the way she wanted it—the way it had to be. She couldn't afford to let down her guard and fall for him again. It wasn't just her welfare she had to think about anymore. Her child was counting on her to make responsible decisions and she wasn't about to let her son or daughter down.

She was going to protect them both from the heartbreak that she feared would accompany her becoming involved with Nate again. It would be better for their child to never know what it was like for his or her parents to be together, rather than go through the upset when they eventually broke up.

Jessie took a deep, shuddering breath. She just hoped she could remain strong and not give in to the temptation of starting something again with Nate that she knew he either couldn't or wouldn't commit to.

The following evening, Nate yawned as he carried a tray with a big bowl of popcorn, a bottle of water for Jessie and a soft drink for him into the media room. He'd spent the entire night lying awake, thinking about the woman in the bedroom across the hall from the master suite. Holding her while they danced at the Broken Spoke, feeling the slight bulge of her rounded stomach rubbing against his lower belly and knowing it was his baby she was carrying had revved his engine faster than he could slap his own ass with both hands.

It was an entirely new experience for him to get turned on by a pregnant woman. That fact alone had caused him to question his sanity more than once. But it was the memory of the lovemaking that had created their child that sent him into the master bathroom for a cold shower in the middle of the night and again early that morning.

Jessie was the most exciting woman he had ever known and having her with him was heaven and hell rolled up into one very enticing little package. He wanted to hold her and show her how good life could be for them. But how was he supposed to convince her that he could be what she wanted him to be if she kept him at arm's length and didn't tell him what it was she wanted?

That afternoon he'd ridden to the south pasture with his men on the pretense of moving a herd of heifers, but the entire time he'd been thinking about what he had to do. At some point, he was going to have to tell her about what he had done to land himself and Sam at the Last Chance Ranch. Then if she could get past that, he needed to find a way to convince her to let him do what was right and marry her.

"Rosemary told me the two of you had a nice little talk this afternoon," he said, setting the tray on the coffee table in front of the leather sofa.

Jessie nodded. "While you and your men were moving your cattle into another pasture, Rosemary and I talked about how different things are now for new mothers than when she had her babies."

"Oh, yeah?" Lowering himself onto the couch beside her, he shook his head. "I wouldn't think there were too many variations on something like being a new mom."

"You'd be surprised," she said, laughing.

The delightful sound sent a wave of heat straight to the region south of his belt buckle. But more than that it gave him hope. Jessie had apparently started to relax and he took it as a good sign that her guard was coming down.

Whether it was that knowledge or the lighthearted mood, Nate grinned. "Are you going to tell me how it's different or are you going to make me guess?"

"I should make you guess." The twinkle in her violet eyes caused the heat inside him to increase. "Your answers might be very interesting."

"You want to shoot me a break here, darlin'?" He laughed. "You know as well as I do that I don't know beans from buckshot about this stuff."

She smiled. "Rosemary and I discussed some of the things that have been developed over the past thirty years to make things easier to care for a baby."

He scooped a handful of popcorn from the bowl to keep from reaching for her. "Let me guess. She compared the way she did it in the good old days to what women are doing today and found the new way lacking."

"Not at all. Rosemary said she wished she'd had all the items available that new mothers have today when she had her first child," Jessie answered as she reached for some popcorn.

"Wow! Whatever these things are, they must be pretty impressive," he said, picking up the remote control. "We'll have to make a trip to one of the baby stores so you can show me all these new gadgets."

"Why do you think they have to be something special?" Jessie asked as she opened the water.

When she put the bottle to her mouth to take a drink, Nate had to stifle a groan. The memory of how those soft, perfect lips felt on his skin caused his heart to race and made it feel like the temperature in the room had gone up at least ten degrees.

"Nate, are you all right?" she asked, her expression concerned.

"Uh, yeah," he lied, popping the top on the soft drink can to take a big gulp. "I'm fine. Why?"

"Aside from the fact that you looked like you might be in pain, you didn't answer my question," she explained.

Oh, he was in pain all right. But it wasn't the kind

she was thinking about. Having her with him and not
being able to hold her, kiss her, was about to kill him.
He had always thought she was pretty, sexy and a lot
of fun to be with, but he had to admit that they hadn't
spent a lot of time together that hadn't involved making love. Now that they were spending time where he
had to concentrate on more than mind-blowing sex,
he was starting to pay more attention to how percep-
tive she was and how much he enjoyed her intellect.

When she continued to stare at him, he forced himself to focus on what she'd said. "I was just trying to
imagine what could have made that big of an impression on Rosemary. She doesn't put her stamp of ap-
proval on just anything."

"Well, she seemed to like the convenience of the
forehead digital thermometers and the video baby mon-
itors." Jessie smiled. "And she especially liked the idea
of electric breast pumps."

"A breast pump?" he asked, sounding like a damned
parrot. He wasn't sure he even wanted to know how
those things worked. "I'm sorry I speculated."

"Don't tell me you find talking about breast pumps
embarrassing," she teased.

"To tell the truth, I really never gave something like
that a second thought." Nor was he sure he wanted to.

It wasn't exactly the subject that made him uncomfortable, it was the fact that he just flat didn't know
anything about taking care of an infant. As he started
the movie and they settled back against the soft brown
leather couch cushions, he decided it might not be a
bad idea to start a list of things he needed to research

on the internet before the baby was born. He'd taken his turn babysitting his niece and nephews on occasion, but they had been several months old and it had only been for a few hours at a time. If he was going to do this "dad" thing right, it appeared that he needed to learn a whole lot more about newborns and their care. Unlike his biological father, he wasn't going to mess things up and fail at something this important.

About halfway through the fast-paced comedy, he noticed Jessie start to yawn and without a second thought, he put his arm around her. When she leaned back to stare up at him, he thought she might pull away, but to his relief she drowsily rested her head against his shoulder and in no time he could tell by her shallow breathing that she was sound asleep.

He smiled. It was further proof that she was definitely letting down her guard with him. Now all he had to do was make sure he didn't become impatient and push for more before she was ready. Considering all he could think about was how sweet her kisses were and how responsive she was when they made love, that was going to be damned hard to do. But he had too much riding on the outcome of her month with him to screw up things with Jessie this time around.

When the movie ended, Nate was reluctant to let her go. Instead of waking her to go upstairs to bed as he should have, he turned the television to the late-night news and continued to hold her. As he sat there pretending to watch what the meteorologist predicted for the next few days, he thought about the woman in his arms and the baby she carried. Wondering if he could feel the baby move, he placed his hand on her stomach and waited.

"It's not unheard of, but I think it's a bit too soon for you to be able to feel movement," Jessie murmured.

"But you can feel him?" he asked, leaving his hand on her stomach. At least he was touching her, even if it was several inches below where he'd like his hand to be resting.

She nodded as she sat up straight. "At first I wasn't sure because it was just a light fluttery feeling."

Nate had never wondered when a pregnant woman felt a baby move. But he was finding there were a lot of things he had never thought about before that had become very important since Jessie had announced he was going to be a daddy.

"How long ago was that?"

"I first noticed it about three weeks ago and then it gradually became stronger and more frequent." She smiled. "Now it's starting to feel a little more like she's gently nudging me."

"And that doesn't hurt or make you feel sick?" If he had something moving around inside of him, he was pretty sure he would be as sick as a five-year-old kid after eating a full bag of Halloween candy.

Instead of answering his question, she used her index finger to poke him just above his navel. He immediately started laughing and caught her to him to keep her from doing it again.

"Not fair." He grinned. "You know that's the one place I'm ticklish."

"You wanted to know how it felt," she answered, her laughter joining his. "I just thought I'd show you."

As he held her close and their eyes met, their smiles faded. "I want to kiss you, Jessie."

"That wouldn't be a good idea," she said, her voice soft and not at all discouraging.

"Do you want me to kiss you, darlin'?" he asked, cupping her cheek with his palm.

"No."

He kissed her cheek and the tip of her nose. "I've never known you to lie before."

She stared at him for what seemed like an eternity before she answered. "Nate, there are times when what we want and what's best for us are two different things."

If there had been any question that she was afraid he would hurt her again, it had just been answered. He could have kicked himself for causing Jessie so much heartache, but he couldn't change that now. All he could do now was move forward and make sure that it didn't happen again.

"Darlin', I know that I've been a thoughtless bastard and you have every right not to want anything to do with me," he said, choosing his words carefully. "Believe me, if I could go back and do things different, I would. But all that's in the past now and besides, circumstances have changed. All I can do is give you my word that it will never happen again."

"Because of the baby," she said slowly.

When he nodded, Nate watched her catch her lower lip between her teeth to keep it from trembling and knew she was fighting to keep her tears in check. It tore him apart to think he was the reason behind all of her turmoil. It reminded him of the times before her death that he had witnessed his mother cry over something his father had said or done. He might not know what a lifetime commitment was all about, but he knew for damned sure it shouldn't be filled with stress and uncertainty. Nate silently made a vow to do everything in his power to never cause Jessie that kind of emotional pain again.

"N-Nate, we went over this before," she said, her voice shaky.

When a lone tear slid down her cheek, he wiped it away with the pad of his thumb, then gently kissed where it had been. "I know we covered this the other day and I asked you then to let me prove to you that I can change. But I can't do that if you won't let me hold you or kiss you. I need to be able to show you, Jessie."

She closed her eyes as she murmured, "N-Nate, I'm tired of your on- and off-again games."

"I know, darlin'," he said, pulling her more fully against him. She was wary and he couldn't blame her. He held her for several long seconds as he tried to find the words to get her to take a leap of faith. "I'm sorry for the way I treated you in the past and I'll be the first to admit that I should be shot for doing that. But I'm in unfamiliar territory here and trying to do what I think is right. All I can do now is ask that you forgive and trust me."

"That's asking a lot," she said, opening her eyes to stare up at him.

He nodded as he leaned forward to kiss her cheek. "I know it's going to take a lot of courage, Jessie. But you'll never know for sure if you don't take the chance. Give me that much and I swear you won't be sorry you did."

The look in her eyes told him she was still frightened, but to his relief, when he slowly began to lower his head, she didn't pull away. Lightly brushing her perfect mouth with his, Nate wondered how he had been able to stay away from her for the past several months.

He felt that way every time he went back to ask her to give him another chance and he briefly wondered if he would get antsy again when things started getting more serious than he intended. But he was going to have to push that concern aside. He was determined to do the right thing and marry her, just as his foster father would expect him to do. But he couldn't help but worry about the next step. What if she pushed *him* aside once she learned what had landed him and his brother in foster care when they were kids and the reason behind it?

Soft and sweet, her lips clung to his and he forgot all about his reservations. When he deepened the kiss to explore her tender inner recesses and reacquaint himself with the taste of her passion, she brought her arms up to circle his shoulders. It caused his heart to beat double time and his breath to lodge in his lungs when she kissed him back. Savoring her like a fine wine, he leisurely stroked her tongue with his as he imitated a more intimate union.

His body began to tighten predictably. Deciding it would be best to end the caress before he took things too far, he started to ease away from the kiss. It appeared she was going to give him another chance and he wasn't going to blow it. Besides, he was only adding more tension to his already frustrated libido.

But apparently Jessie had other ideas and, suddenly taking control, she did a little exploring of her own. Nate's body hardened so fast it caused him to feel light-headed and, groaning, he had to shift to keep his jeans from emasculating him.

"I think it's about time for me to walk you upstairs to your room," he said as he tried to force air back into his lungs.

Everything in him urged him to kiss her again and with a lot more passion. But he couldn't risk doing something stupid now. Not when one wrong move could give her reason to end things between them for good.

When they climbed the stairs and walked to her bedroom, he kissed her cheek, stepped back and started back downstairs. "Sweet dreams, darlin'."

"Aren't you going to bed now?" she asked.

Turning back, he shook his head. "I've got a rodeo coming up and I need to put in some time in my workout room."

"Thank you for inviting me to go with you this coming weekend." She gave him a smile that set his pulse to racing as she opened the door. "I'm looking forward to seeing you ride."

He nodded. "I'm looking forward to having you there with me."

As she went into the room and closed the door, he realized it was true. He was anticipating having her watch him ride. It was something he had avoided because he had wanted to keep things light between them and not make her think they were becoming a couple.

But at the moment, that was the last thing on his mind. He had a fire in his blood that only Jessie could put out. And since making love to her wasn't an option just yet, he fully intended to exhaust himself. Maybe then he would be able to get some sleep.

Heading back downstairs, Nate went straight to the workout room and, taking off his shirt, picked up a twenty-five pound weight and started doing bicep curls at a furious pace. He had enough adrenaline flowing through his veins to bench-press a tractor and considering all he could think about was the woman upstairs, it was going to take a minor miracle to work off that kind of rush.

A half hour later, when he climbed the stairs and walked down the hall to his room, Nate stopped to stare at the closed door across the hall. He knew for certain he was destined for another fitful night. All he could think about was having Jessie in his bed, holding her and loving her until the break of dawn. His body immediately began to tighten and burn with a need that was all too familiar.

"Son of a bitch," he muttered, resigned to the fact that he was once again going to suffer through a shower cold enough to freeze the balls off a pool table.

Four

As Jessie and Nate started up the steps of the grandstand at the rodeo in Amarillo, he reached out to take her hand in his and the warmth that flowed through her from the contact was breathtaking. Since their talk a few nights ago, he had taken every opportunity to remind her of how things could be between them with tender touches and kisses that left her weak and trembling. But she hadn't had to stop him from going too far. She could tell he wanted more, but true to his promise, he wasn't pushing her further. The only problem was, it was becoming a true test of her resolve not to ask him to. This was the longest they had gone without making love and she missed the intimacy between them.

When they reached the seating area where the families of the contestants and rodeo personnel sat, Jessie was happy to see Summer and Bria waving to her and Nate to get their attention. At least she would have someone she knew to sit with and talk to while she waited for Nate to compete in the bull and bareback riding events.

"I didn't know your brothers and their wives would be here," she commented as they reached the row of seats where the women sat with their children.

"Ryder is one of the bullfighters and Sam is the stock contractor," Nate answered as he pushed his wide-brimmed Resistol back on his head. Putting his arms around her, he gave her a quick kiss. "I hate to just walk you up here and leave, but I've got to register and see what my draws are."

She frowned. "Your draws?"

"The bull and horse I'll be riding today," he said, grinning.

"I think I need a crash course in rodeo terminology." Knowing he needed to register for the events he would be competing in, she smiled. "Go ahead and do what you have to do. I'll be fine here with Bria and Summer," she assured him. "I'm looking forward to talking to them again."

"I'll see you after the bull riding," he said, giving her another kiss.

As Nate turned to go back down the bleacher steps to find the registration office, Jessie made her way to the empty seat beside Summer and her little girl, Katie. "It's good to see I've got you two to explain what's going on," she said when she sat down.

"Is this the first time you've seen Nate ride?" Bria asked.

Jessie nodded. "I usually have to work weekends."

She didn't want to explain that this was the first time Nate had asked her to watch him in the two and a half years they had been seeing each other. For some reason it just seemed a little embarrassing to admit she obviously hadn't meant that much to him.

"Have you already taken your maternity leave?" Summer asked, shifting her sleeping daughter from her shoulder to her lap.

"No, I took some vacation time to stay with Nate until Thanksgiving," she admitted. Explaining his requests, she added, "Given our past history, I'm still not sure I'm doing the right thing."

"I can understand your reservations," Bria said, her tone sympathetic. "He's been extremely inconsiderate in the past and you have every right not to trust him. But I don't think you have to worry. Deep down Nate really is a good guy and he'll be great with the baby." Grinning, Bria added, "However, when it comes to your relationship with him, you're in charge now. Don't hesitate to make him grovel a few times. He definitely deserves it."

"Bria's right," Summer agreed. "He does deserve a hard time. But I've never known any of the six brothers to go back on their word. If Nate says he wants to marry you and make a life for the baby, I can guarantee he means it."

Jessie had no doubt that Nate would be a good father. He was great with his niece and nephews, and she was confident that he would love their baby. But it was the way he felt about her that kept her awake at night. Had she set herself up for another fall?

He had a track record when it came to their relationship and it wasn't a good one. And even though she had agreed to let him show her how it could be between them, she didn't hold out a lot of hope that he wouldn't lose interest in her as he'd done before.

That was why while staying out of his bed might be extremely difficult for her, it was for the best. If they made love, she knew she'd fall for him all over again and that's something she just couldn't allow herself to do. It was her job to protect the baby, but she also needed to protect her heart as well. Unfortunately, when it came to Nate, she didn't seem to have a lot of choice in the matter. From the moment they met, he had been her biggest weakness and it appeared that he always would be.

"Jaron's competing today as well as Nate," Bria commented when the announcer acknowledged the cowboys competing in the day's events who had already qualified for the National Finals in Las Vegas.

"Is Mariah going to be here to watch him?" Jessie asked.

Bria shook her head. "He's never asked her and she wouldn't even if he did. She refuses to watch Jaron ride—especially the bulls. She's afraid he might be injured and she can't stand the thought of seeing that happen."

"I can understand how she feels," Jessie admitted. "I'm nervous about watching Nate climb on the back of any animal with nothing more on its mind than throwing him off so it can stomp on him."

Summer sighed. "I know what you mean. Even though he doesn't ride and I've seen him save cowboys from being injured more times than I can count, I still hold my breath whenever Ryder jumps in front of a bull to distract it."

"How much longer is Ryder going to work as a bullfighter?" Bria asked. "I know he's cut back a lot since Katie was born and only works the rodeos Nate and Jaron compete in."

"He says he'll give it up completely once they stop riding." Summer gave Jessie a reassuring smile. "Even though it makes me nervous, my husband really is one of the best at what he does. He'll move heaven and earth if he has to in order to make sure Nate and Jaron don't get hurt. And if that means risking his own safety, that's what he'll do."

Bria nodded. "Sam told me that all of the bull riders breathe a little easier when they know Ryder is working the event."

Nate had told her several times that his brother Ryder was one of the bravest men he'd ever known and had a protective streak a mile wide when it came to those he loved. Knowing that he was in charge of keeping the men safe did make her feel a little more relaxed about the bull riding. But as a nurse, Jessie had seen some of the damage those animals could do to the human body and the thought of something like that happening to Nate or any of the brothers scared her as little else could.

When the rodeo began Jessie did her best to relax and enjoy the timed events. She couldn't believe how fast some of the cowboys were at roping and tying a calf or how quickly cowgirls could race their horses around barrels without falling off.

"The bareback event is next," Bria said, glancing at the program. "Nate and Jaron will both be riding in this one."

"The horses aren't as dangerous as the bulls are they?" Jessie asked, hoping that was the case.

Bria shook her head. "If a cowboy is thrown before the eight-second horn goes off, the horse doesn't turn back and try to hurt him."

Several contestants attempted to ride the horses they had drawn for the event—some of them even successfully—before Nate was announced as the next rider. From their seats in the grandstand they had an excellent view of the riders climbing onto the backs of the animals, and Jessie found herself sitting on the edge of her seat when the light gray horse Nate was attempting to mount reared up in the chute.

"Does that happen often?" she asked, alarmed. As she watched, the chute crew helped Nate reposition himself on the horse's back as if it was no big deal.

"There are some horses that have a bad habit of doing that in the bucking chute and the gate men know to put a rope on the horse to keep it from rearing up and injuring itself or the rider," Bria said, frowning. "But this is the first time I've seen Silver Streak do that. Normally he waits until he gets out into the arena to cut loose and go wild."

Jessie had forgotten that Sam was the stock contractor providing the livestock for the different events. Of course, Bria would be familiar with all the animals and their particular habits.

Once Nate was settled on the back of the animal, he nodded his head and a man on the outside of the bucking chute swung the gate open. The horse jumped straight up, then seemed to explode out into the arena kicking and pitching sideways as it tried to throw Nate from its back.

"Silver Streak is outdoing himself," Bria said excitedly. "If Nate can hang on for the full eight seconds, he's going to get one of the highest scores of the day."

"How do you know?" Jessie asked, breathing a little easier when the horn signaled that eight seconds were up and two cowboys on saddled horses rode up beside the bucking animal for Nate to dismount safely.

"Fifty percent of the score is based on how well the horse bucks and the other fifty is based on how well the cowboy rides it," Summer explained. "Silver Streak did everything he could to buck Nate off. But Nate did an excellent job of riding the horse for the full eight seconds."

Summer had just finished her explanation of the scoring system when Nate's score was announced over the loudspeaker. Compared to the scores of previous riders, his was by far the highest.

"That's going to be hard to beat," Bria said, smiling.

"I'm sure the cowboy who's about to ride will try," Summer said, laughing when Jaron's name was announced.

"Is there a big rivalry between Nate and Jaron?" Jessie asked, feeling a sense of pride at Nate's accomplishment.

"All of the guys are very competitive," Bria answered. "But they're all proud of the others' accomplishments as well."

Summer nodded. "If Nate wins, Jaron will be the first one to congratulate him, the same as Nate will do if Jaron wins."

"I love the way they're all so supportive of each other," Jessie said, meaning it. Coming from a family that had never encouraged a strong bond, she envied them.

"They've all been through a lot together and I vowed when I married Sam to help them stay close," Bria admitted. "That's why we have so many parties and family dinners. It's a good way for them to maintain the bond they formed as teenagers."

"I love that Katie and I are part of it all," Summer stated, smiling. "I went from having no siblings to having this wonderful, loving family that made me feel like I'd always been part of them." She reached down to squeeze Jessie's hand. "You and your baby are part of that now, too."

"Thank you," Jessie said, blinking back tears as they watched the rest of the rodeo.

She really didn't see how she could be considered one of them if she and Nate weren't going to be together. But it was a real comfort knowing that her child would have the love and acceptance of such a wonderful extended family.

By the time the bull-riding event started, Jessie had relaxed a little more. But as Nate climbed onto the back of the big, mean-looking bull he'd drawn, her body tensed involuntarily. Unable to watch, she closed her eyes to keep from seeing him be hurt.

She opened her eyes in time to see Nate dismount and fall to his knees. Thankfully the animal proved to be fairly docile. Instead of seeking revenge, the bull trotted out of the arena without even bothering to look Nate's way. That eased her mind a little; now all he had to do was ride two more bulls over the next couple of days without being injured and she would be able to relax completely.

After a nice dinner with his brothers and their wives, Nate carried his and Jessie's bags into the hotel lobby and stopped at the front desk. They were late checking in and he hoped they could get squared away without too much hassle. The drive up to Amarillo had taken a lot longer than he had anticipated because of traffic tie-ups on the interstate due to construction, and they hadn't had time to stop by and check into their rooms before he had to be at the rodeo arena to register for his events.

"I have two rooms reserved for the next three nights," he said, approaching the front desk. When the desk clerk looked up, Nate gave the man his name and waited while he keyed in the information on his computer.

"I'm sorry, Mr. Rafferty, we only have you down

for one suite for the three nights," the guy said, shaking his head.

"Is something wrong?" Jessie asked, walking up beside him.

"They only have one room reserved for us," he said, barely resisting the urge to cuss a blue streak. She was never going to believe that it was the hotel's screw-up and not him trying to pull a fast one on her. It wouldn't be the first time he'd arrived at a hotel to find there had been some kind of computer mix-up. Of course, because of his VIP status with the hotel, they usually bent over backward to accommodate him. But he'd just as soon not deal with any kind of issues if at all possible.

"But you told me you were getting two rooms," she insisted, her tone a little suspicious.

"I did." He reached into the hip pocket of his jeans to fish out his wallet. Removing his identification and the hotel's VIP card, he pushed them across the counter toward the man squinting at the computer like it held the secrets of the universe. "Please check your files again. I booked one suite online over three months ago and I called at the beginning of this week to book another."

Without comment the man keyed the information into the computer, then after clicking the mouse a couple of times and keying in more information, he looked up. "I think I know what happened. Whoever you talked to when you called to make your reservation for the second room put you into the system as wanting one suite with two beds, instead of two suites with one bed."

Nate shook his head. "Whatever. I need two suites."

The guy shrugged as if he didn't know what else to do. "I'm sorry, but I can't give you another room because we're booked solid. The rodeo is in town."

Nate rolled his eyes and pointed to the fringed leather chaps draped over his arm. "I know the rodeo is in town." He looked at the man's name tag. "But that doesn't solve our problem now, does it, Ralph? I'd really hate having to stay elsewhere from now on because you aren't able to accommodate my request."

Ralph quickly shook his head. "That won't be necessary, Mr. Rafferty. I'll see what I can do, but because of the rodeo being in town…"

"Yeah, I got that, Ralph. The rodeo is in town." Nate took a deep breath as he tried to hold on to his patience. "Just check to see if there's any way you can accommodate my request."

"Nate, let's just take the suite he has reserved for you," Jessie said, surprising him.

"Are you sure?" he asked.

Since their talk a few nights ago, things had been going along pretty well between them and he'd like to keep it that way. But staying in the same room with Jessie, even if it was a suite, sleeping so close to her and not being able to make love to her would be like playing with a stick of dynamite. It was bound to get him into trouble and damned quick.

"I'm tired and I'm sure you are, too," she said, nodding. "As long as there are two beds, it shouldn't be an issue."

A sudden wave of heat surged through his body and he gritted his teeth as he turned back to the desk clerk.

Sharing a room might not be a problem for her, but it sure as hell would be for him. Unfortunately, staying in the same suite seemed to be their only option.

"We'll take what you have," he finally said, knowing he would be completely insane by morning.

"Would you like help with your luggage?" Ralph asked as he handed Nate a couple of key cards.

"No, I'll take care of our bags," Nate answered as he signed for the room.

A few minutes later, as he and Jessie rode the elevator to the fourth floor, Nate couldn't help but wonder if having to sleep in such close proximity to Jessie instead of with her was his penance for the way he'd handled their relationship over the past two and a half years. If he thought he'd gone through hell the past several days with her in the room across the hall from his, he couldn't imagine what it was going to be like sleeping just a few feet away from her. He was pretty sure he already had frostbite from freezing his ass off every night in a cold shower. How on God's green earth was he going to make it through the next few nights without turning into an icicle?

"This is nice," Jessie said, oblivious of his inner turmoil when he opened the door to their room. "These are amazing." She touched the expensive silk comforter on one of the beds. "Which one do you want?"

The one you're going to be in. "It doesn't matter to me," he answered. Setting their luggage on the floor in the bedroom, he hung his chaps on the valet stand, then turned to watch her walk around the room. She stopped at the balcony doors to look out at the brightly lit Amarillo skyline. "This room has a great view."

"It's a nice city," Nate agreed, continuing to watch her. He could tell she was a little nervous about the arrangement and trying to put her at ease, he pointed to the minibar. "Would you like something to eat or drink?"

"We just had dinner with your brothers and their wives."

"I heard you tell Bria and Summer that you're always hungry," he said, grinning. "I just thought you might need a snack before we turn in."

"I think I'm going to shower, then go on to sleep," she said, unzipping one of her two bags.

He picked up the huge television's remote control. "I think I'll watch a little TV. Will that bother you?"

As she dug through the bag to find whatever she was looking for, she shook her head. "No, but go ahead and watch whatever you like. It won't disturb me." She laughed as she straightened with a hot-pink nightshirt in one hand and a zebra-striped toiletry bag in the other. "I think I proved the other night when we were watching the movie that I can sleep through whatever is on the TV, even if it's something I want to see."

He barely managed a smile as she turned to go into the bathroom. All he could think about was her taking off her clothes to get into the shower and him joining her. His body tightened to an almost painful state when he remembered the times they had showered together over the past couple of years.

Clenching his jaw so tight it would take a crowbar to

pry it open, he sat down on the end of one of the beds and took off his boots. How the hell was he going to get through one night of being in the same room and not being able to make love to her, let alone three?

"Nate, could you please check to see if there are extra pillows on the closet shelf?" Jessie asked as she came out of the bathroom several minutes later.

He did his best not to stare as she walked over to the bed to put the clothes she'd been wearing before her shower into her suitcase. The hot-pink nightshirt she wore wasn't even remotely sexy under normal circumstances. It hung all the way to her knees, was completely opaque and couldn't have been more shapeless. But that didn't seem to matter. Just knowing that she probably didn't have anything on under it besides her panties had him feeling like a range-raised stud seeing his first filly.

"Are you all right?" she asked when he continued to stare.

"Just peachy," he muttered, swallowing back a groan.

"Could you check the closet?" she asked again.

"Uh, right. Pillows." Focusing on her request, he looked inside the closet and shook his head. "No extras. Why do you need them?"

"I forgot to bring the wedge pillow," she said, frowning. "I always put that under the side of my stomach and another pillow against my back."

"You can use one of mine," he offered, knowing it wouldn't matter how many he had. He wasn't going to get any sleep anyway.

"Or you could call the front desk and have one sent up to the room," she suggested.

He shook his head. "I only need one anyway."

"Are you sure you don't mind?" She continued to rearrange her clothes in the suitcase. "You need your rest if you're going to compete tomorrow."

If he hadn't found the situation so dismal, he might have laughed at her erroneous assumption that he'd be able to relax enough to sleep. But there wasn't anything funny about being aroused for a week. He had finally broken down and found his own relief, but that was always hollow and only relieved his physical discomfort. It did absolutely nothing to alleviate the emptiness he felt not having Jessie in his arms.

"I think I'm going to take a shower now," he said, unsure of how many more cold showers his traumatized body could endure. Grabbing a change of underwear from his duffel bag, he motioned toward the bed he knew for certain he would lie awake in for the entire night. "Go ahead and take both pillows if you need to."

He hoped by the time he got out of the shower, Jessie was in bed, covered up to her ears and sound asleep. When he came back into the room ten minutes later with his teeth chattering like a set of fake choppers from a novelty shop, he shoved his clothes into his duffel bag and turned to find her snuggled up in a nest of bed pillows. Unfortunately, she was still wide awake.

"Can't...sleep?" he asked, trying not to shiver.

"I can't get comfortable," she said, sitting up.

He frowned. "Is something wrong with the bed?"

She shook her head as she punched the pillow she'd

had at her back. "No, the bed is fine. It's the pillows. They're too soft. They flatten out when I lean back against them."

"Is this a pregnancy thing?" he asked, wondering if it was for her comfort or had something to do with the health of the baby.

"Yes," she said, punching the pillow again before she gave up and tossed it back onto his bed. "Since I'm on my feet so much when I'm working at the hospital, I'm trying to make sure I protect and rest my back muscles as much as possible."

"Is that because your stomach is getting bigger?" he asked, figuring the bigger a woman got the more extra strain it put on her back.

Nodding, she pushed her silky blond hair out of her eyes. "And I've already started wearing a maternity support belt when I work."

He wasn't even going to speculate on how that little jewel was worn or what it did. Just the name of it suggested that something was uncomfortable. The thought that he was responsible for Jessie experiencing any discomfort made him feel guilty.

"I'm sorry, darlin'," he said, sitting down on the side of her bed.

She looked confused. "What are you apologizing for?"

"If I hadn't made you pregnant, you wouldn't be having all these problems with your back," he said, feeling a lot like a fish out of water. He really needed to research what she was going through and what he could do to help make things easier.

Instead of accepting his heartfelt gesture, she laughed. "Nate, I'm not having back issues. Yet. What I'm doing now is preventive." Smiling, she placed her hand on his forearm, sending a shockwave coursing throughout his body. "And even if I do start having backaches in the last few months of my pregnancy, it will all be worth it once I hold the baby."

The realization that she was looking forward to having his baby, instead of viewing the unplanned pregnancy as a mistake, caused a warm feeling to spread throughout his chest. "You really mean that, don't you?"

"Of course," she said, placing her hand on her rounded stomach. "Why wouldn't I?"

He shrugged. "Since I wasn't exactly your favorite person when you discovered you were pregnant, I wasn't sure how you'd feel."

"No matter what happened in the past or will happen in the future, it doesn't change the way I feel about our baby," she said, her tone serious. "I might not have planned this, but I've loved this child since the moment I learned I was carrying her."

"Or him," he said, grinning. "We won't know the gender for another week."

"As long as he or she is healthy, I really don't care," she said firmly.

Staring at her, he surprised both of them when he motioned toward the middle of the bed. "Move over."

"Nate—"

"I'm going to be your back support," he said, easily lifting her to the center of the mattress.

All things considered, he was probably out of his mind to think that he could hold her all night without losing what little sense he had left. But she needed her rest and he was going to see that she got it, no matter what kind of hell he had to go through.

When he stretched out beside her, Nate turned onto his side, then pulled her back against his bare chest. "Is that comfortable?" he asked as she arranged one of the pillows under the side of her belly.

"Yes, thank you." She suddenly went perfectly still. "Why are you so cold?"

"I had to take a shower," he said truthfully.

"A cold one." Her tone indicated she knew exactly why. "Maybe you supporting my back isn't such a good idea." She sounded sleepy and not all that convincing.

"It feels good, doesn't it?" he asked, nuzzling the side of her neck. Her silky hair against his face felt like heaven and he didn't think twice about leaning over to kiss her cheek.

"Mmm-hmm," she murmured, snuggling into him.

"Then don't worry about it, darlin'," he said, feeling his body start to react. He took a deep breath and tried to relax. "Nothing is going to happen unless it's what you want, too."

"Even though it frightened me, I liked…watching you ride…today," she whispered sleepily. "You're very… good."

Before he could tell her that he was sorry he hadn't asked her to watch him before and that just knowing she was in the stands was all the incentive he needed to make a better ride, Nate could tell by her even breathing that she had fallen asleep. Kissing the side of her head, he closed his eyes and willed himself to relax.

Even though he wanted her more than he wanted his next breath, he could feel himself start to get sleepy and briefly wondered if he was just that exhausted or if it was due to the fact that he had her in his arms. But as he lay there enjoying her soft body against his, an unfamiliar protectiveness settled over him. And his last thought as he finally drifted off into the first peaceful sleep he'd had in a week, was that he would move heaven and earth to keep this woman in his life and in his bed, even if he was scared spitless that he was going to screw things up.

Five

On Sunday afternoon, Jessie sat in the rodeo grandstand with Bria, Summer and their children, watching the bulls being loaded into the bucking chutes for the bull-riding event. Nate had made it through the past couple of days unscathed and won the right to compete in the final round. Now if he could just get through this ride without being hurt, she could breathe a little easier—at least until the next time he climbed onto the back of one of the ill-tempered beasts.

As she continued to watch the activity around the bucking chutes, Nate walked into view and her breath caught. He was without a doubt the sexiest cowboy she'd ever seen. Wearing a Western-cut red plaid shirt with the long sleeve rolled up to the biceps on his riding arm to keep it from getting caught in the bull rope, her heart skipped a beat. His muscles were strong, well-defined and felt absolutely wonderful wrapped around her as they slept.

Thinking about the past two nights, her chest tightened with emotion at how solicitous he had been. Each night he had let her rest her back against his chest and snuggle close to him. And she knew what a sacrifice that had been on his part. She'd felt his arousal several times against the back of her upper thighs, but he'd been a perfect gentleman and hadn't tried to coerce her into making love. He'd told her nothing would happen unless she wanted it to and he had been true to his word. The only problem was, she had struggled both nights to keep from turning to him, to once again feel the strength of his lovemaking.

It was so tempting to throw caution to the wind and give in to what she knew they both wanted. But she had to stay strong, and not just for her or the baby's sake. She had to consider the effect it would have on Nate as well. She could tell he was trying so hard to make this work between them—something that he'd never done before. If they made love again and he discovered that he couldn't commit to anything long-term, she knew for certain he would end up hating himself for hurting her again. Rather than allow that to happen, it was better for all concerned if they didn't go there at all.

"Nate's up next," Bria said, bringing Jessie out of her musings.

"What kind of temperament does the bull have that he'll be riding?" she asked, hoping the animal wasn't as mean as some of the others she'd seen.

Bria winced. "I'm afraid the bull he's riding is known for wanting to hook a rider with his horns."

Jessie gasped. "Please tell me you're joking."

"Don't worry, Jessie," Summer said, grabbing her hand to give it a gentle squeeze. "Ryder will be there to turn the bull when it's time for Nate to dismount safely."

Unable to take her eyes off Nate climbing over the side of the chute to ease himself down onto the back of the bull, Jessie could only nod as she continued to hold Summer's hand. Her gaze riveted on him, she held her breath when he leaned back slightly, gave a short nod of his head to signal he was ready and the gate to the chute swung open wide.

The bull immediately jumped straight up, then bumped into the chute as it bucked its way out into the arena. Lurching and twisting, the animal seemed to pull out all the stops to get the man off its back before it settled into a dizzying spin as if chasing its own tail. When Nate started to slip sideways, Jessie was certain her heart quit beating until he managed to straighten himself back onto the middle of the animal's broad back.

When the horn blared, signaling the eight seconds were up, everything seemed to move in agonizingly slow motion. Ryder ran forward to gain the bull's attention so that Nate could dismount, but she knew instantly that something was wrong. He continued to hold on to the bull rope as he slid to the bull's side.

Jumping to her feet, she covered her mouth with her hand to hold back her scream. Terror like she'd never known flowed through every vein in her body at the sight of Nate being dragged like a rag doll while the bull continued to buck. She wanted to do something to get Nate away from the furious animal, but all she could do was watch helplessly as Ryder ran along on the opposite side of the bull, trying to free Nate's hand from the rope.

"Nate's gone down in the well," Bria said, her expression worried. "He's hung up in the bull rope and can't get to his feet."

Both Bria and Summer were used to seeing all kinds of things go wrong during the rough-stock events and if the women were upset, Jessie knew it had to be bad.

Another bullfighter did his best to distract the beast as Ryder worked to untangle Nate's hand, but when it finally slipped free and he slumped to his knees on the dirt floor of the arena, Nate didn't get up and sprint to the fence like he'd done after his other rides. While the other bullfighter managed to entice the bull away from Nate, she watched Ryder kneel down beside him and Jaron run over from the chutes to see what was wrong. Her heart sank when Ryder and Jaron both motioned for the Justin Heelers to enter the arena.

Knowing the medical team would get him out of the arena and take him to a triage area to assess his injury, Jessie turned to Summer. "Where will they take him?"

"Follow me," Summer said, picking up her daughter's diaper bag and starting down the steps of the grandstand. As a former public relations director for the rodeo association, she led them to the area behind the chutes where several officials stood. "Where's the training room?"

"Sorry ma'am, but y'all can't go back there," one of the older men said, shaking his head. "It's authorized personnel only."

"Try and stop me," Jessie stated determinedly.

"If you need authorization, talk to Sam Rafferty about his wife and sisters-in-law going into the training room to check on his injured brother," Bria said, stepping forward. "I'm sure he'll tell you that it would be highly inadvisable to try to stop us. Now get out of the way."

The man looked at the two women holding sleeping babies, then at Jessie, who was obviously pregnant. He immediately stepped out of their path, having decided it wasn't worth the fight. "It's the second door to the right, Ms. Rafferty," he called after them as they hurried down the corridor.

When they reached the training room, Summer motioned toward an open door down the hall. "We'll wait for you in the press room."

"Thank you," Jessie said before hurrying in.

Entering the training room, Jessie was relieved to see Nate sitting up on a cot with his legs stretched out in front of him. One of the medical staff was using a pair of scissors to cut the right leg of his jeans from the hem up to the knee. When the man peeled back the blood-soaked denim, she could see that Nate had a deep laceration on his calf, but otherwise looked to be all right.

"I'm fine, Jessie," Nate said quickly when he looked up and saw her.

"What happened?" she asked as her gaze traveled from his head to his feet to make sure the cut was his only injury.

"My leg got caught between Whiplash and the latch on the gate when he left the chute." He shrugged. "It isn't the first time I've needed stitches after a ride."

If she could have gotten closer to him, she would have bopped him on top of the head. She had been worried to death about his welfare and he was dismissing the incident as no big deal.

"How does your arm feel?" she asked, knowing that it had been under a major strain when he was hung up in the rope.

"It'll be okay." He winced when he tried, but failed to lift it above his head. "It's sore, but nothing that an ice pack won't fix."

"You're lucky it wasn't dislocated at the shoulder." She made it over to a chair in the corner to sit down when her knees began to wobble. Now that she'd seen Nate was going to be all right, the adrenaline started to wear off and she was as weak as a newborn kitten. "And don't you dare say it wouldn't be the first time you had a shoulder injury," she warned. "It's the first time I've ever seen you get hurt and it's a very big deal for me."

He stared at her for a moment before asking the man cleaning the wound on his leg to give them a moment. "Come here, darlin'." When she walked over to him, he pulled her down next to him. "Jessie, I'm sorry. I forgot that this weekend was the first time you've seen me ride. Are you all right? You aren't so upset that it's causing you problems, are you?"

"I think I was frightened out of at least a year or two of my life, but other than that, I'm okay," she assured him.

He used his index finger to lift her chin until their eyes met. "I'm going to be just fine. A few stitches or a dislocation are just part of being a rodeo rider."

Before she could tell him how glad she was that he hadn't been seriously injured, he leaned in close and the moment his mouth covered hers, she forgot all about the rodeo, bulls or where they were. All she could do was feel the warmth flowing through her from being held by him again.

When he deepened the kiss she put her arms around his neck and, kissing him back, instantly felt a need begin to build inside her that only Nate could ease. She wanted to once again feel his strength surround her and feel the gentle power of his lovemaking.

"Well, I see that you can't be too bad off," Ryder said, laughing.

At the sound of Nate's brother's voice, Jessie tried to pull away from him, but he tightened his arms around her to hold her to him. "Thanks for saving my bacon out there, bro. I owe you one."

"All in a day's work," Ryder said, walking over to get a chemical ice pack from one of the shelves. "They don't call me Dances With Bulls for nothing. But you're wrong about owing me one. It's more like you owe me a dozen or so."

"Who won the round?" Nate asked.

"Jaron took first and you got second," Ryder said, activating the ice pack to place it on his knee. After wrapping an Ace bandage around it to hold it in place, he started toward the door. "He and Sam will be coming to see about you as soon as Sam makes sure his wranglers get the livestock loaded up and Jaron collects your and his winnings from the pay window."

When the doctor walked back into the room, Jessie stepped away from the cot. "I'm going to go find Bria and Summer while the doctor finishes cleaning your leg and sutures the laceration." It was a good excuse to escape and regain her equilibrium. Turning back, she advised the doctor, "While you're at it, you might want to check his shoulder. I think it might be partially separated."

"She's a registered nurse down in Waco," Nate said when the doctor raised an eyebrow. "If she says to check it out, you'd probably better do it."

The doctor nodded. "An observant nurse is worth her weight in gold."

"I'll see you in a little bit, darlin'," he said, giving her a look that made her insides feel as if they had turned to warm pudding.

As she walked down the hall to the media room where Summer and Bria waited, Jessie knew that she was quickly approaching the point with Nate where she was going to have to make a decision. She was either going to have to trust that Nate wouldn't lose interest in her this time and resume their relationship, or end things between them for good before she lost her heart to him completely. And no matter how many times she told herself to stay strong, she knew it wasn't going to do any good.

Unfortunately, she was afraid the die had already been cast. If she wasn't already head over heels in love with him again, she didn't have far to fall.

"Jessie, I swear I've got this," Nate said, refusing to allow a woman to carry her own luggage. Especially one who was five months pregnant. His foster father would roll over in his grave if Hank knew one of the boys he finished raising wasn't sticking to the Cowboy Code, even if it was because of an injured shoulder and a gimpy leg.

"Nate, you didn't want me driving the three hundred miles from Amarillo after you took pain medication, but I managed that." She gave him a pointed look. "Trust me, I'm perfectly capable of carrying at least one of the two small overnight cases."

Dropping both of their bags, Nate wrapped his good arm around her and kissed her until they both gasped for breath. "Give it up, darlin'. I'm getting the luggage. You just open the door for me."

She stared at him for several seconds before she sighed. "All right. But when we get into the house, I want you in bed with that leg elevated and ice on your shoulder. You don't want to make things worse by ignoring doctor's orders."

"Is this Jessie the bossy nurse talking?" he asked, grinning as he bent down to pick up both bags with his good arm.

"Yes." She opened the door leading from the garage into the mudroom. "And you're going to find out just how mean and bossy I can be if you don't do what I tell you."

"Do you want to play nurse and patient after we go to bed?" he teased as they walked into the kitchen. "I can let you adjust my arm sling and check my stitches right after you give me a bed bath."

Rolling her eyes she shook her head. "You're incorrigible."

"You can't blame a guy for trying," he said, laughing.

"Nate, being injured is serious," she said, turning to frown at him. "If you don't take care of your shoulder, you could cause permanent damage to the tendons and ligaments."

"Shh. You'll wake Rosemary," he said, knowing that a bomb could go off outside her bedroom and the woman would snore her way right through it.

He had hoped to divert Jessie's attention. The tactic failed.

"I still don't see why we couldn't have spent the night in Amarillo and come back here in the morning as we'd planned to do," she whispered as they walked down the hall and started up the stairs.

"I have approximately three weeks to get this shoulder straightened out before National Finals in Las Vegas," he explained when they reached their rooms. "I've got a physical therapist on retainer and he can be here tomorrow morning to start my rehab exercises. I want to get the jump on this because if I don't I might as well skip Vegas and stay home."

"You've been hurt so many times you have a concierge physical therapist?" she asked, her expression disbelieving as she opened the bedroom door. "How did I not know that?"

"I guess I just got hurt during the times when we weren't seeing each other," he said evasively, carrying her bag over to set it on the bed. He didn't want to tell her that several of the times he had been injured it had been right after he broke things off with her and he'd had his mind on her instead of being focused on his riding.

She started to dig through her suitcase, presumably for her nightshirt. "Well, don't forget to prop your leg up and put ice on your shoulder for about twenty minutes before you go to sleep."

Setting his duffel bag on the floor, he reached for her. "I'm going to need your help," he said, pulling her to him.

"What on earth for?" she asked, sounding delightfully breathless.

"I have a registered nurse staying with me and you expect me to do all this medical stuff on my own?" he asked, kissing the satiny skin along the side of her neck. He nibbled at the hollow behind her ear. "I think you should sleep with me in my bed tonight so you can take care of me and make sure I'm all right."

"Really? You're going to use that excuse?" she asked, shivering against him.

He nodded. "I might not get the pillow in the right position when I prop up my leg. Or the ice pack might slip off my shoulder and I wouldn't be able to put it back in the right spot."

She leaned back to look up at him. "Nate, I don't think—"

"I served as your backrest for the past two nights," he reminded her.

"That's not fair," she said, her expression not nearly as disapproving as he was sure she meant it to be. "Those pancakes the hotel was passing off as pillows were too flat to serve as any kind of support."

"I can't help it if I got used to holding you while we sleep," he said, tracing his finger down her delicate cheek. "Besides, darlin', I hate to admit it, but I'm hurting too bad right now to do anything anyway. And once I take another pain pill, I'll be zonked out in no time." When she began to nibble on her lower lip, he knew she was going to give in. "Come on, Jessie. Didn't you like being snuggle buddies?" He used his thumb to stop her from worrying her lip, then gave her a gentle kiss. "I know I sure liked it."

She closed her eyes and nodded. "All right. But just for tonight."

"Why don't we just take it one day at a time and see how long I need you with me?" he suggested, knowing that once he got her in his bed he intended to make sure she stayed there.

"Nate, where is your arm sling?" Jessie asked when she sat down on the couch and noticed that he wasn't wearing the stabilizer.

"I've graduated to Kinesio tape," he answered

proudly. He stopped watching the crime show on the big-screen TV in his media room to lift the sleeve of his T-shirt. Two strips of the brightly colored support tape used by a lot of athletes ran from his shoulder down to his biceps. He was fortunate that it had only been a partial separation and not a complete dislocation or a break. And she was certain the injection the doctor had given him to reduce inflammation had helped tremendously.

"I've always been amazed by how fast a good physical therapist is able to get results," she said, happy to hear Nate was progressing so quickly. It had only been five days since Max, his physical therapist, had showed up to start working with Nate on his rehab exercises. "Does he think you'll be ready to take part in the National Finals next month?"

Nate smiled. "Yup. Max says I'll be ready a few days before I have to be in Vegas. That will give me a chance to ride a couple of Sam's practice bulls to get back in the swing of things."

Jessie forced a smile. "That's nice. You'll have to tell me all about the finals when you get back." It was a complete lie. She didn't want to think about him riding another ornery animal—not even for practice— or that he might get hurt again while he was doing it.

"I won't have to tell you about it," he said, smiling as he shook his head. "You'll be right there with me."

She stared at him for endless seconds and tried to stay calm. "I really don't think I can do that, Nate," she said, choosing her words carefully.

He frowned. "Why not, darlin'?"

"I'll be working at the hospital in Waco by then," she said, thinking quickly. "And I can't use any more of my vacation days or else I won't have any extra time to take off when the baby is born."

"Don't worry about time off without a paycheck," Nate replied as if it didn't matter that she wouldn't have money to pay her rent. "I'll take care of whatever you and the baby need."

"Excuse me?" She wasn't sure she had heard him correctly. "You're absolutely not going to pay my bills." It would make her feel like a kept woman to have him taking care of her expenses.

"Calm down, Jessie." He took her hands in his. "I'm just telling you that I want to make sure you have as much time with the baby as you'd like before you go back to work. I know how important that is to you and I'm going to make sure that it happens."

It was true that she was determined to keep her financial independence, but there was more to her reaction than that. The main reason she was so upset had nothing whatsoever to do with her going back to work or him paying for her to stay home with the baby. It was all about his week and a half at the rodeo National Finals in Las Vegas and the danger he would face on the meanest bulls the stock contractors had to offer. Not to mention that she was overly tense from the frustration of spending every night lying in bed with him snuggled against her. Since their night in Amarillo the longing had built inside her and she felt as tightly wound as a coiled spring.

"Can we discuss this later?" she asked suddenly.

If they continued to talk about it, she was afraid she would end up telling him the real reason she wouldn't be going to watch him ride—that she was scared to death she'd see the man she was falling for get hurt again or worse.

Nate continued to stare at her for a moment before he finally nodded and put his arms around her. "I don't want you to worry, Jessie—not about having extra time with the baby or about me getting hurt when I'm riding the bulls. Stress isn't good for you or the baby."

She didn't even try to correct him about his assumption that she was frightened he would be injured again. They'd both know she would be lying if she did.

"That's easy for you to say. You aren't the one having to watch and know that there's nothing you can do to stop the disaster happening right before your eyes," she said, giving up all pretense about what the real issue was that had her so upset. "You weigh about a hundred and seventy pounds. Those bulls weigh two thousand. When it comes right down to it, who do you think will be the first to break?"

He leaned back to look at her. "Are you telling me you want me to quit?"

Upset and unable to sit still, she rose to her feet to pace the room. What did she want? Nothing would please her more than to know he was never going to risk his life on the back of another one of the vile animals. But just because she wanted that, didn't mean it was right for him. That was his decision to make, not hers.

She took a deep, steadying breath. "I would never

ask you to do that, Nate. You're a bull rider. It's what you do. It's who you are. And I know you're good at it."

He continued to sit on the couch, staring at her. "You've always known I ride the rough stock, Jessie. I told you that up front the day we met."

She stopped pacing to look directly at him. "Knowing what you do is one thing. Watching you do it is something else entirely."

"I understand you're concerned that I might get hurt," he said calmly. "But I know what I'm doing, darlin'. I've been riding bulls for almost twenty years and I'll admit that I've had a few close calls. But in all that time I've only been seriously injured once."

As far as she was concerned that was one time too many. But she refrained from telling him that. She still wasn't sure where things were going with them and didn't feel she had the right to ask him to give up riding, even though her heart was telling her that was exactly what she wanted. If he quit, it had to be because it was what he wanted. Not because it was something she wanted him to do.

"I understand that, Nate." She shook her head. "I'm just telling you I can't watch you."

He got up from the couch to walk over and put his arms around her. "Why does the possibility of seeing me get hurt bother you so much, Jessie?"

His deep baritone and the feel of being wrapped in his strong arms caused tears to fill her eyes. Unwilling for him to see how emotional she was about the subject, she laid her head against his broad chest.

"I don't like seeing anyone hurt, Nate," she hedged.

"Being a nurse, I've seen how truly fragile the human body can be."

"You didn't answer my question, darlin'," he persisted, kissing the top of her head. "What bothers you so much about the idea of me being hurt?"

She knew what he wanted her to say—knew that he wanted her to reveal how she truly felt about him. But she wasn't ready for that. She wasn't ready to admit, even to herself, just how much he really meant to her. If she did that and he didn't feel the same way about her, she would only be opening the door for more heartbreak. She had done that too many times before and each time she had been devastated when it didn't work out between them. The last time, she hadn't been sure she would make it until she discovered she was pregnant. And as crazy as it sounded even to her, she had taken comfort in the fact that if she couldn't have Nate in her life, she would at least have his child.

"I think I'm going to go upstairs," she said pulling from his arms. She needed time to come to terms with the fact that she was so very close to falling in love with him again—if she hadn't already. "I'm really tired and I'd like to be rested up for the drive down to Waco tomorrow to have the ultrasound."

Walking from the media room without looking back, Jessie knew Nate watched her leave. She was grateful that he hadn't tried to stop her, even if a small part of her was disappointed that he hadn't.

Six

Sitting in the waiting room next to Jessie, Nate watched several pregnant women and their partners being called back to the examination rooms and wondered if the guys felt as clueless about all this as he did. He'd done a little research on the internet about what a woman went through as the baby grew inside her and how her body changed, but he couldn't say it felt all that real to him.

Maybe he hadn't come to terms with the fact that he was going to be a daddy. He still couldn't feel the baby move when Jessie told him to put his hand on her rounded stomach. When was a man supposed to feel a deep emotional connection with his baby? Was he the only guy to feel like he was part of something that he couldn't quite get a handle on? Or was he destined to be like his biological father—a man who was incapable of feeling anything that didn't benefit him in some way or hadn't come out of a whiskey-soaked haze?

The thought that he might turn out to be cut from the same cloth as his worthless father was Nate's worst nightmare. Joe Rafferty had been an abject failure at being a husband and father, and the day he walked out to leave his two sons on their own after their mother died had been the luckiest day of their lives.

They'd had to resort to armed robbery just to survive. But even that had turned out to be a lucky break for them. After getting caught, they had been placed in the care of Hank Calvert and during their stay at the Last Chance Ranch, they'd learned what it meant to be honest, law-abiding men.

His brother Sam had turned out to be a great husband and father despite the early example their father had set for them. But Nate had yet to prove himself. Could he live up to the standard his brother had set? Could he be the man he'd always hoped he would be?

"Jessica Farrell?" a woman in a white lab coat called from the door leading back to the examination rooms.

Brought back to the present, Nate rose to his feet and took Jessie's hand in his as they walked down a hall to the room where the ultrasound would be done. He had no idea what he was supposed to do, but he figured holding her hand for moral support was a good start.

"I'm Dr. Evans," the woman said, introducing herself to Nate.

"Nate Rafferty, ma'am," he said, removing his Resistol and extending his hand.

The doctor smiled as she shook his hand. "Are you two ready to find out if you're having a boy or girl?"

"I've been waiting for this day since I discovered I was pregnant," Jessie answered, sounding excited as they entered a small room.

When the doctor looked at Nate expectantly, he didn't know what else to do but nod. He wasn't about to explain that he had only learned about the baby a couple of weeks ago or that he hadn't quite wrapped his mind around the idea that he'd fathered a child.

"If you'll help Jessica up on the table, we'll get started and take the first pictures of your baby," the doctor said, closing the door and seating herself on a stool beside a machine with a small television screen. "Dad, you can stand on the other side of the table in order to get a better view of the screen."

Helping Jessie up onto the small bed, he took his place where the doctor had indicated as he tried to take in the woman's use of the term *dad*. But before he had the chance to let that sink in, Jessie raised her red maternity top and eased her slacks down to reveal her stomach. He had felt the firm bump when he held her against him and the few times he'd put his hand on it when he'd try to feel the baby move, but she hadn't actually shown her stomach to him. He'd seen her beautiful body many times before, but that had been before she'd become pregnant. Was she self-conscious now about the changes in her body?

She had no reason to be. She was more beautiful now than he'd ever seen her.

When Dr. Evans squeezed some clear jellylike stuff

from a tube onto Jessie's stomach, then picked up something that looked like a microphone, Nate reached down to take hold of Jessie's hand. He wasn't sure if it was for her moral support or his. All he knew was that it felt as if he was about to witness something very profound and something that would change his life forever.

With the first touch of the instrument to the clear gel on Jessie's stomach, the screen displayed a shadowy image. For the life of him, Nate had no idea what he was supposed to be looking at.

As the doctor continued to slide it around on Jessie's abdomen, she pointed to the machine. "There's your baby's profile," she said, smiling.

His gaze riveted to the screen, Nate's breath lodged in his lungs when he recognized a little head and an arm and leg. The world suddenly seemed to stand stock-still and reality hit him right square between the eyes. That was his baby he was watching—the child he had made with Jessie.

He glanced down at her lying on the table. Tears had filled her violet eyes and the most beautiful smile he'd ever seen curved her perfect lips. At that moment, he wasn't entirely sure he didn't have a tear or two trying to escape his own eyes.

"Does everything look all right?" Jessie asked.

"Everything looks just fine," Dr. Evans assured her, nodding. "It appears that your baby is right on target for a twenty-week-old fetus, both in size and development."

"That's wonderful," Jessie said as one of her tears slowly trickled down her lightly flushed cheek. He gently wiped it away with his index finger, earning a smile from her. "Is the baby turned so that you can see the gender?" she asked.

Dr. Evans moved the probe around a moment before she grinned. "Well, it looks like you're going to be buying a lot of pink and purple. There's no doubt about it, this baby is most definitely a little girl."

"I'm having a girl," Jessie murmured like she couldn't quite believe it.

When she looked up at him with such excitement and wonder on her face, he didn't think twice about lowering his head to kiss her with all the emotion he was feeling but couldn't put a name to. At that moment, Nate felt like beating his chest and doing the Tarzan yell. He was going to be a daddy and it suddenly became more important than ever to make sure Jessie and the baby stayed with him—not just for the rest of the month or the first year of the baby's life. He wanted them with him from now on.

He had to get past his concern of turning out like his miserable old man and be there for them through thick and thin—to protect them and take care of them.

"I'll get some pictures ready for you," Dr. Evans said quietly as she handed Jessie some tissues to wipe away the remaining gel. She clearly knew how special the moment was and didn't want to intrude.

Once Jessie had cleaned away the last traces of the gel and rearranged her clothes, Nate helped her off the table. "Is there anything else we need to do?" he asked.

"No. I'll see you in a couple of weeks for your regular appointment," the doctor answered as she handed Jessie the pictures and opened the door to precede them out into the hall. "And you know if you have any problems, I want you to call my office or go straight to the ER."

"What did she mean by that?" Nate asked. He didn't remember Jessie mentioning anything other than morning sickness in the early weeks of her pregnancy. "Is something wrong? Have you been having problems? Is there something we haven't been doing that we should?"

"Calm down," Jessie said as they walked out the doors of the clinic to his truck. "I haven't had any issues, nor do I expect any. And for that matter, neither does Dr. Evans. She frequently reminds all of her patients to seek medical attention if they do experience something out of the ordinary or that they're concerned about."

Nate breathed a little easier after Jessie's explanation, but it appeared he needed to put in a lot more time on the computer. There was a whole hell of a lot more he needed to learn about what a woman went through during pregnancy, not to mention what was happening with the baby. And the sooner he got started the better.

"Did you get finished doing whatever you needed to do on the computer?" Jessie asked Nate when they walked into the media room after dinner. From the time they returned from having the ultrasound in Waco until just before dinner, he had been sequestered in his office, working on what she assumed to be ranch business.

"Not quite," he said, picking up the remote from the coffee table.

"Is there anything I can help you with?" she offered as she sat down on the couch.

Turning on the television, he shook his head. "I've only got a few more things I need to read up on." He sat down beside her and put his arms around her. "Have I told you lately how beautiful you are?"

"Where did that come from?" she asked, laughing self-consciously. "How did we go from talking about what you're doing on your computer to how you think I look?"

His sexy grin made her feel warm all over. "I turned the computer off, darlin'." He kissed her forehead, cheek and the tip of her nose. "But seeing you sitting here looking so damned irresistible turns *me* on."

"It doesn't take much for that to happen," she teased, loving the look of appreciation in his dark blue eyes.

"You've always had that effect on me," he said, his expression turning serious. He brought his hand up to cup her cheek. "From the first time I met you, I wanted you." He lightly brushed her lips with his. "You excite me in ways that I could have never imagined."

The sincerity in his tone and the desire in his eyes stole her breath. Over the past week she had lain in his strong arms each night, felt the evidence of his need and known the toll it had to be taking on him. For that matter, it had become exceedingly more difficult for her as well. She longed to once again have him join their bodies, to feel the exquisite power of his lovemaking and bask in the intimacy of being one with the man who meant so much to her.

When Nate lowered his head to cover her mouth with his, it didn't occur to her to resist. She wanted his kiss, wanted to lose herself in his gentle caress. As his lips moved over hers, she lifted her arms to thread her fingers in the light brown hair at the nape of his neck and gave herself up to the feelings only he could awaken in her.

A delicious warmth spread throughout her body when he deepened the kiss to stroke her inner recesses with such tenderness it made her feel as if she might melt into a puddle. She had always responded to his mastery, but each time he kissed her, the need inside of her became more intense than anything she could ever remember.

Tightening his arms around her, he took her with him when he stretched out on the couch and, partially lying on top of him, she immediately felt his arousal as it strengthened with every beat of his heart. Her own body answered with an empty ache deep in the most feminine part of her. Whether it was due to the fact that they had shared a very poignant moment during the ultrasound or due to her crazy pregnancy hormones, she wanted nothing more than for him to make her his once again.

She knew she would have to put aside all of the things that had been holding her back and that she might very well end up getting her heart broken again. But as one of her coworkers always said, the heart wants what it wants. And her heart wanted Nate.

"I think we'd better…stop this before I do something that's sure to…get me into big trouble," Nate said, sounding as short of breath as she felt. He moved her to his side and turned to face her. "Right now, I want you more than I want my next breath and as bad as I hate to say this, it might be best for you to sleep across the hall tonight."

The warmth inside her increased and her pulse raced. "Is that what you want me to do?"

"Hell, no!" He laughed as he shook his head. "What I'd like to do is to take you upstairs right now, remove every stitch of your clothes and spend the entire night making love to every inch of your delightful body."

Her heart skipped a beat and she had to remind herself to breathe. "Then why don't you?" she asked before she could stop herself.

A deep groan rumbled up from his chest a moment before he leaned back to look at her. "Jessie, I'm not in any shape right now to be a gentleman. The past week has done a real number on my nobility and willpower. If you don't mean what you just said, then it would be a real good idea to put some distance between us right about now."

Reaching up, she cupped his lean cheeks with her hands. "I don't want to move away from you, Nate. I want to be so close to you that our hearts beat as one."

He closed his eyes for a moment and she watched a nerve jerk along his jaw. "Are you sure about this?"

"Yes," she said decisively. She would face whatever consequences her actions caused later. At the moment, being in Nate's arms, having him love her as only he could was all that mattered.

"Let's go upstairs, darlin'," he said, getting up to help her from the couch.

Neither spoke as they walked out of the media room, across the foyer and up the stairs. Words were unnecessary. They both knew what they were about to do was the next step in resuming their relationship and whether it worked out for them or not, Jessie knew in her heart she would regret it for the rest of her life if she didn't give them the chance to find out.

He put his arm around her shoulders as they went down the hall to the master suite and once the door was closed behind them, he took her in his arms for a kiss that left her weak in the knees. When she sagged against him, Nate swung her up in his arms to carry her across the sitting area to the king-size bed.

"From what I've read, it should be safe for us to make love," he said, setting her on her feet. He reached up to trace her jaw with his index finger. "But I want to make sure, darlin'. Did Dr. Evans mention anything that might indicate we shouldn't?"

"No." His concern was touching. "As long as we aren't rough, everything should be fine."

He chuckled as he lifted her maternity top up and over her head. "No wild, swing-from-the-rafters-like-a-monkey kind of sex, huh?"

She smiled. "I don't recall you and I ever engaging in anything like that before."

Shaking his head, he kissed her collarbone as he unfastened the clasp of her bra. "That's never been my style, darlin'. I've always preferred taking my time and loving every inch of you."

A shiver of anticipation coursed through her as he slid the lacy straps from her shoulders and tossed it aside. "I've always thought your body was beautiful," he said, his tone husky as he cupped her breasts in his calloused palms.

She knew her body looked vastly different than it had the last time he'd seen it and although she felt sexy and took pride in her impending motherhood, she had heard that some men found it to be a turnoff. "A lot of things have changed because of the pregnancy," she said, feeling a little self-conscious.

"I noticed that at the doctor's office today," he said, nodding. When he kissed each of her breasts, then raised his head, the look in his eyes made her feel like the most cherished woman alive. "Maybe it's because it's my baby you're carrying, but I've never seen you look more beautiful than you do right now."

His heartfelt compliment caused a lump of emotion to clog her throat and she raised up on tiptoes to press a kiss to the steady pulse at the base of his neck. "You look pretty good yourself, cowboy," she said, loving the look of sincere appreciation in his dark blue eyes.

She had always thought Nate was the sexiest, best-looking man she'd ever met and no matter how many problems they'd had in the past couple of years, that hadn't changed. Something told her it never would.

Kneeling in front of her, he removed her slippers, then his gaze captured hers as he hooked his thumbs in the waistband of her maternity jeans to slowly, carefully lower them and her panties. Jessie braced her hands on his wide shoulders as she stepped out of the garments and watched him toss them on top of the rest of her clothes.

Her breath caught when he placed his hands on either side of her stomach and leaned forward to kiss the taut skin. "You've always been the sexiest woman I've ever known." There was a reverence in his voice that left no doubt in her mind he meant every word he said.

Rising to his full height, he reached for the lapels on his chambray shirt, but stepping forward, Jessie brushed his hands away to stop him. "Let me."

He nodded. "I'm all yours, darlin'."

She unfastened the snap closures to press her lips to the newly exposed skin. "I love your body," she said as she continued kissing her way down his chest. By the time she reached the well-defined muscles of his abdomen, his breathing sounded extremely labored. Glancing up, she asked, "Are you all right?"

His charming grin sent a wave of heat flowing through her veins. "If I was any better, I'm not all that sure I could stand it."

When she tugged his shirt from his jeans and pushed it off his shoulders, she placed her hands on his broad chest. "I love how hard your muscles are," she said, touching the thick pads of his pecs.

He shuddered when she used her index finger to trace each flat male nipple. "Keep that up and the show will be over before we ever get started," he said, capturing her hands in his. "I promise that next time you can take off all of my clothes," he said, stepping back to unfasten the button at the waistband of his jeans. He quickly removed his boots and, carefully unzipping his fly, shoved the denim and his boxer briefs to his ankles. Stepping out of them, he kicked them toward the pile of clothes on the floor. "It's just been too damned long since I made love to you, darlin'," he said, reaching for her.

The feel of his hair-roughened male flesh meeting her softer feminine skin sent a wave of need from the top of her head all the way to the tips of her toes. It seemed as if it had been an eternity since Nate had held her body to his without the encumbrance of clothing and she longed for an even closer connection.

"Please, Nate," she said, trembling with desire to be one with him. "I…need you. Now."

"Where?" he asked, brushing his lips over hers.

"Inside," she whispered.

Without another word he lifted her to the middle of the bed then stretched out beside her. Taking her in his arms, he gave her a kiss that made her feel as if she might burn to a cinder.

"We may have to be a little creative with the position," she whispered, hoping he understood. The changes in her body also dictated a change in the way they made love.

"That's why you're going to be on top this time," he said, nibbling kisses along her collarbone a moment before he turned to his back. When he lifted her over him, the promise in his blue gaze caused her heart to beat double time. "We'll figure out more positions later. Right now, I need to be inside you, darlin'."

As she took him in, Jessie closed her eyes at the overwhelming feelings of joy spreading throughout her body from their coming together once again. She never felt as complete as she did when she and Nate made love, and she'd missed being part of something that felt so perfect, so right.

When she opened her eyes, he was looking at her with such tenderness that she teared up. "I've missed you, Jessie," he said, his voice hoarse with need as he cupped her face with his palms. "Take me with you, darlin'."

Unable to remain passive any longer, she began to move in a slow rhythmic motion against him. All too soon, the pleasurable tension holding them captive began to build toward the peak of fulfillment and Jessie tightened her body around him to prolong the enchantment.

Nate moved his hands to her hips and she could tell by the look on his handsome face that he was fighting the same battle she was. They both wanted their joining to last, but the lure of mutual satisfaction was too strong a force to resist.

All too soon the tight coil of need within her let go its grip and, crying his name, Jessie gave herself up to the waves of pleasure coursing through her. Her gratification must have triggered Nate's because she felt him surge into her one final time then hold her to him as he filled her with his essence.

When she collapsed on top of him, Nate gently lifted her to his side to wrap her in his strong arms. As he cradled her to him, she knew in her heart that she loved him—had never stopped loving him.

But as she floated back to reality, the uncertainty of their circumstances returned full force. Had she further complicated an already complex situation?

After watching the wonder on his face when they saw their baby for the first time on the ultrasound, she had no doubt that he would be a good father and always be there for their daughter. Unfortunately, she still had her doubts about him losing interest in his relationship with her. Everything was fine for now. But they had been down this road before. Things would be going great between them and he'd suddenly decide that they needed to take a break.

There was so much she was risking that it was overwhelming. She had laid her heart on the line again. What if Nate wasn't able to work out whatever issues he had about commitment? He had said he was ready to take that step and wanted them to get married, but of all the times he mentioned loving the baby, she couldn't remember a single time that he had mentioned loving her. Could she take that leap of faith, knowing that he might never give her his heart as fully as she gave hers to him?

And then there was the risk of his job. She wasn't sure her nerves could take watching him ride bulls, knowing what the price of a single mistake could be. She would never ask him to give up such a big part of who he was just because she was frightened of what might happen to him. But she wasn't sure she could live with the risk of him being seriously injured or worse.

"What's wrong, Jessie?" he asked gently, tipping her chin until their gazes met. "I didn't hurt you, did I?"

"No," she said, shaking her head.

"Then why are you crying?" he asked, wiping the moisture from her cheek.

"Th-that was beautiful," she said, thinking quickly. She hadn't even realized she was crying.

She wasn't exactly lying. Their lovemaking had always been meaningful. But she wasn't going to tell him that it wasn't the reason for her tears.

"You're beautiful," he said, smiling. He kissed her with a tenderness that caused a fresh wave of emotion to fill her eyes. When he raised his head, he frowned. "*Now* why are you crying?"

"P-pregnancy hormones," she stammered, not entirely sure they weren't partially responsible for her unsettled feelings.

He surprised her when he nodded. "I've heard they can cause mood swings."

"Where did you hear that?" she asked, grateful for the distraction from her earlier thoughts.

He chuckled as he tucked her to his side and reached to turn off the bedside lamp. "When my sisters-in-law were pregnant, my brothers all stashed tissues in their pockets like a miser stashes away cash."

Yawning, she nodded. "That was probably a good idea."

"I think I'll get a few of those pocket packs to carry with me the next time I go to town," Nate said, grinning.

"Another…good idea," she agreed as sleep began to overtake her.

Nate listened to Jessie's even breathing for several minutes to make sure she was asleep before he arranged a pillow behind her back for support and eased himself out of bed. Gathering his discarded clothes from the floor, he tossed them into the hamper before entering the bathroom for a quick shower.

Ten minutes later, he pulled on fresh jeans and a T-shirt, checked to make sure Jessie was still asleep and headed back downstairs to his office. He had spent the entire afternoon reading everything he could find online about pregnancy and a baby's development. There were a few more things he needed to check out before he felt like he might have a grasp of what he could do to make things easier for Jessie through the next several months as well as what he could expect during the baby's birth.

Picking up the pictures on his desk that the doctor had printed from the ultrasound, Nate stared at the image of his daughter. *His daughter.*

He swallowed hard. He was going to have a little girl. Just the thought caused his stomach to ache and his head to pound. When she got old enough to date, how in the hell was he going to keep teenage boys like he had been away from her?

A protectiveness suddenly came over him that he'd never experienced before. Now he understood what Ryder had meant about making sure he was cleaning his guns whenever Katie started dating and some pimple-faced boy came around the Blue Canyon Ranch to pay her a visit. Ryder was hoping just the sight of a couple of rifles and a shotgun or two would scare the kid into being a gentleman. Nate decided right then and there to file that idea away for future reference when his daughter got old enough for boys to start hanging around the Twin Oaks Ranch.

Turning on the computer, he took one last look at the image of his baby girl before propping it up against the monitor and opening the internet browser. He might be scared half out of his mind of all the things he would face being the father of a daughter, but he was going to protect Jessie and his little girl in every way he could. They were counting on him and he wasn't going to let them down. He was going to get his act together this time and do things the right way or die trying.

Seven

When Jaron dropped by the following afternoon, Nate took him to see the new herd of Black Angus cattle he and his men had moved to the south pasture a couple of weeks ago. "I'll be adding a herd of working horses after the first of the year." Nate propped his forearms on the gate as they watched the stock graze on the thick Bermuda grass.

"You'll need them," Jaron said, nodding. "When we were helping you stretch new fence last spring, I noticed you have a couple of places on the eastern side of the ranch that are so grown up with scrub and downed trees they're only accessible on horseback."

"Yeah, over the years storms have taken down a lot of trees and the previous owner wasn't all that interested in cleaning them up," Nate explained. "I've got clearing those areas on the to-do list for next spring and summer." He shrugged. "That's if there's enough time to get to them between cutting and putting up hay in the barn for next winter and everything else that we'll have to do."

"You know who to call if you need some extra hands to get it all done," Jaron stated. It didn't surprise Nate that Jaron had volunteered himself and the rest of their brothers to help out. All any of them had to do was pick up the phone and they would be there in a heartbeat to lend a hand.

"What about rodeo?" Nate asked. "The summer schedule is the busiest time on the circuit. How are you going to juggle competing and helping me get all this stuff done?"

"I'm going to cut way back on the number of events I enter this next year—if I compete at all." Shrugging one shoulder, Jaron gave a half smile. "The competition is getting younger, the bulls are meaner and I'm looking at getting out before I get hurt too bad to enjoy my retirement."

Nate knew what his brother meant. He was thirty-three and Jaron was thirty-four. Once a rough stock rider turned thirty, the clock started to tick. Between the inevitable injuries, and the wear and tear of competition taking a toll on a rider's body, he had five or so years left that he would be healthy enough to compete at the world-championship level. As with any other highly physical professional sport there were exceptions to the rule. But not all that many.

"I've been giving it some serious thought the past

week or so myself and I'm thinking about hanging up my chaps and spurs after the finals this year," Nate said, staring out across the pasture. "I figure I'd rather go out a winner than a has-been."

Jaron nodded. "That's what I've been thinking. I'll bet Jessie's happy about your decision. I know she was pretty upset when you got roughed up in Amarillo."

"I haven't told her yet," Nate said, shaking his head. "But I don't think she'll be sorry to hear it." They were silent for a time before Nate admitted, "Finding out that I'm going to be a daddy has been a game changer for me. Jessie and the baby are going to need me and I'm determined I'm not going to let them down. I can't be there for them if I'm too gimped up to get around."

"I was wondering if that might not have played a big part in your decision," Jaron admitted.

Nate knew his brother would understand. Like Nate and Sam's, Jaron's father had been anything but a positive role model for his son.

"I know a lot of other riders have wives and kids and don't think twice about competing in the rough-stock events." Nate shook his head. "But you and I have watched a couple of friends die in past years because of wrecks in the arena and I want to make sure I don't put Jessie and our daughter through that."

"The baby is a girl?" Jaron asked, sounding incredulous. When Nate nodded, his brother threw back his head and laughed out loud. "After chasing skirts all these years it's only right that you have a little girl to worry about. Now you'll know what the fathers of all those women went through worrying about their daughters going out with you."

"Yeah, I thought about that." Nate groaned. "I'm pretty sure I'm already well on the way to developing an ulcer just thinking about some skinny-assed kid trying to get her into the back of his daddy's pickup truck for some star gazing."

"Karma's a bitch," Jaron said, grinning. The most serious one of his brothers, it was good to see the man enjoying himself, even if it was at Nate's expense.

"Don't laugh too hard, bro," Nate advised. "You know what Hank always told us about laughing at each other. The very thing you make fun of has a damned good chance of coming back to bite you in the butt." Nate grinned back at his brother. "Like you said. Karma's a bitch."

"Yeah, but unlike you, I didn't try to date the entire Southwest female population," Jaron shot back good-naturedly.

"Hey, in the past two and a half years I've only been with one woman," Nate pointed out. The realization that what he said was true caused the breath to lodge in his lungs. Even when they had broken up he hadn't wanted to date anyone else.

"You should have married Jessie a long time ago," Jaron said, voicing what Nate was sure all of his brothers had been thinking. "She's the only one you ever went back to. That should have told you something."

Nate nodded. "I had my reasons, the same as you have yours for trying to keep Mariah at arm's length."

"Yeah," Jaron agreed as they walked back to Nate's

truck. "I've got too much respect for her to saddle Mariah with that kind of baggage."

Nate knew what his brother meant. They had not only become brothers during their time at the Last Chance Ranch, they had become best friends. Nate was the only one who knew the whole truth about what Jaron had gone through as a kid and the crushing guilt the man carried because of it to this day.

When they returned to the ranch house, Nate followed Jaron as he walked over to get into his truck to leave. "If you don't mind, keep the news about the baby's gender under your hat for a while."

"Hey, it's your news to tell." Jaron chuckled. "Besides, I figure you probably want to avoid the rest of the brothers giving you what for when they find out you and Jessie are having a girl. At least for a while."

"Yeah, I'm going to be a major source of entertainment for you guys for quite some time to come," Nate said, laughing. "But look at it this way. If they're picking on me, they're leaving you alone."

That earned him a big grin from Jaron. "That's what I'm counting on, bro."

Two days after Jaron stopped by the ranch, Nate found himself strolling through the furniture department at one of the baby boutiques in Waco. He felt like a fish out of water looking at all the gadgets and things a baby needed. How could something that tiny need so much stuff?

"I never realized there were so many different styles

of baby beds," he said, stopping to look at a white crib and the one just like it in light oak. "Or colors."

Jessie nodded as she used the scanner the manager had given her to scan the UPC code for the gift registry she was setting up. "I think I'm going with the white furniture. I don't know why, but it seems more girlish than the natural wood."

"Yeah, that oak is about the same color as a baseball bat I used to have as a kid," he agreed. He mentally noted the color and style she liked. He knew a master furniture craftsman and fully intended to surprise her by having the entire ensemble custom made for the nursery.

"Funny you should mention that," she commented as she checked out a rocking chair that matched the white crib. "I had decided to decorate the nursery in a baseball theme if I found out I was having a boy."

"What are you going to use for the theme now that you know we're having a girl?" he asked, picking up a purple unicorn with a rainbow-colored horn.

"I can't decide between ponies or ballerinas," she answered. "Why?"

"I was just wondering if this is something that would go in the nursery and if you think the baby would like it," he said, holding up the stuffed toy for her inspection. "I've never been a unicorn type of guy, but this one kind of grows on you."

Jessie laughed. "I don't think we'll know for a while what she likes."

"I think I'll go ahead and get it," Nate said, tucking it under his arm. When Jessie gave him an indulgent smile, he felt a little self-conscious. "You know, just in case it turns out that she does like unicorns." He wasn't sure why, but he wanted to be the first one to buy something for his little girl.

"I'm sure she'll love anything you get for her," Jessie said, placing her hand on his arm. She stared at the stuffed toy for a moment before she smiled. "You know, I hadn't thought about a unicorn theme for the nursery. But I really like it. Thank you for that."

Nate grinned. "Nice to know I'm good for something besides making you pregnant."

Her expression was thoughtful when she looked up at him and he briefly wondered if he'd said something she took offense to. The websites he visited during his research said that a pregnant woman could be overly sensitive at times and about things that normally wouldn't matter.

"It's kind of rough for dads, isn't it?" she asked, suddenly putting her arms around him to give him a hug. "In a way, I'm sure you feel a little like you're on the outside looking in. All of the changes are happening to me and all you get to do is watch."

He automatically closed his arms around her and thanked the powers that be that he hadn't upset her. "I don't mind too much as long as I get to watch you." Kissing her forehead, he smiled. "It's my favorite pastime."

"I love watching you, too, cowboy." When she stepped away from him, her sweet smile sent his blood pressure soaring. "We'd better get this finished and drive back to your ranch."

"Is there a reason we need to hurry back home?" he asked, watching her scan a car seat and stroller combination before moving on to add a high chair to the items on the registry.

Grinning, she nodded. "I think we need to take a nap."

Confused, he stood in the middle of the baby-mattress aisle for a minute before it dawned on him what she meant. He had also noticed the websites mentioning that during the second trimester some women noticed a decisive increase in their libido because of all the extra hormones. It certainly seemed to be the case with Jessie. She had suggested an afternoon "nap" the past couple of days.

He couldn't seem to stop grinning. He didn't mind at all that she wanted him to take naps with her. Come to think of it, he was feeling a little "sleepy" himself.

An hour and a half later, Nate smiled as they entered the master bedroom and he removed his boots. "Thanks for letting me tag along while you scanned all that stuff at the baby store."

She reached up to put her arms around his neck and he automatically wrapped his around her waist. "I love that you want to be so involved, Nate."

"I wouldn't think to be anything else but involved," he admitted, realizing it was true. "Even if we didn't plan on it happening, we created this baby together. I'm not going to just sit back and let you go through any of this alone. It's a joint effort, darlin'. And like Lane would say in one of his poker games, I'm all in."

"That means so much to me, Nate." The expression

on her pretty face robbed him of breath and he knew without a shadow of doubt that he wanted to be the only man she ever looked at that way.

Before he could process what that might mean, she raised up on tiptoe and gave him a kiss that registered a solid ten on his internal Richter scale. As her soft lips caressed his, her nails lightly grazed the back of his neck and sent a shockwave of heat racing straight to the most vulnerable part of him. Jessie had always had that effect on him and he knew for certain she always would.

"I need you," he said, kissing her lips, her chin and along her jaw to her temple. His voice sounded a lot like a rusty hinge and he was surprised he was able to form a coherent thought, let alone verbalize it.

"I need you, too," she said, sending another wave of heat through him when she kissed the pulse at the base of his throat. She reached to unfasten the snaps on his shirt. "You made me a promise the other night and I'm going to collect on it."

"What was that?" It didn't matter what she wanted. Right at that minute, he'd jump off a cliff if she asked him to.

"You told me that I could take your clothes off of you," she said, grinning.

Nate laughed. "Well, never let it be said that I went back on my word. Have at it, darlin'."

When she tugged the tail of his shirt from his jeans, Nate loved the playful look that crossed her face. Unless he missed his guess, she was going to treat him to a little sensual foreplay and a whole hell of a lot of torment before they made love.

Pushing the shirt from his shoulders and down his arms, he couldn't wait to see what she had in store for him next as she tossed it aside and reached for his belt buckle. He was thankful she made quick work of the leather strap and the button at his waistband. His jeans had become way tighter than what was comfortable and he couldn't wait to get out of them.

But apparently Jessie had other ideas. She toyed with the tab of his zipper a moment before she abandoned it in favor of running her index finger down the metal teeth and back up over his arousal.

He groaned. "You're trying to make me crazy, aren't you?"

"Is it working?" she asked, her smile promising.

Unable to get his vocal cords to work, he nodded.

"You seem to have a problem," she commented as she eased the zipper down a fraction of an inch. "Do you want me to check it out for you?"

Nate forced himself to breathe. "If you don't, I'll be crawling the walls in another minute or two."

Her delightful laughter was like a balm to his soul. "I certainly don't want to be the cause of that," she said, taking the zipper down a little farther. By the time she finally lowered it completely, Nate felt as if every bit of air had been sucked from the room.

But if he had thought she was finished teasing him, he was dead wrong. When she shoved his jeans down his legs and he stepped out of them, instead of taking off his boxer briefs right away, Jessie ran her finger along the top of the elastic waistband, then down the seams of the fly.

Closing his eyes, Nate let his head fall back as he tried to draw in enough oxygen. He wanted to let her take her time and have her fun, but he wasn't sure how much more he could stand.

"Jessie…don't get me wrong…I'm loving everything you're doing to me," he managed to get out as he opened his eyes and his gaze met hers. "But…if you keep that up much longer…I'm going to disappoint both of us."

"Then I suppose I'd better get you out of these," she said, slipping her fingers beneath the elastic band.

Just the feel of her fingertips on his skin was like a lightning strike to his system. In all of his thirty-three years he could never remember being hotter or harder than he was at that moment. His engine was definitely revved and firing on all cylinders. Much more and he was going to explode.

"I really don't know how much more of this I can take," he said, feeling perspiration pop out on his forehead and upper lip.

When she carefully freed him from the black cotton boxer briefs, Nate had had enough. He'd kept his end of the bargain and allowed her to take off his clothes. Now it was time for him to take control.

"Playtime is over, darlin'," he said, whisking her maternity top over her head in one smooth motion. Dropping it on top of his clothes, he unfastened her bra with one flick of his fingers.

"How do you do that?" she asked, sounding as breathless as he did.

"Do what?" he asked, adding the scrap of lace to the pile, then helping her out of her jeans and panties.

"It takes me longer to fasten my bra than it takes you to unfasten it," she said, bracing her hands on his chest as she stepped out of the rest of her clothes.

"Talent, darlin'." He laughed, releasing some of the tension gripping him. "I have a lot of hidden talents."

She glanced down at his aroused body and smiled. "And some that are hard to hide."

Taking her in his arms, he grinned. "Well, you got the hard part right. And no, I don't intend to hide how much I want you." He kissed her as he picked her up. "I don't even want to try. Now, put your legs around my waist, Jessie. We're going to do something you suggested."

She rested her forehead against his as he carried her over to the bed. "We're going to be a little creative?"

He nodded as he sat on the edge of the mattress and settled her on his lap. "This way I get to be closer to you. I can kiss you and hold you to me."

Nate lifted her and felt like he might pass out from the mind-blowing feel of her body consuming his. It was always this way with Jessie. When she held his body inside hers, he felt like he was part of everything that would ever matter to him.

Once she was completely settled over him, he placed his hands on her hips and helped her set a slow, gentle pace. Sooner than he wanted, his focus began to narrow and a red haze clouded his mind. He needed to complete the act of loving her, needed to once again leave a part of himself in her safekeeping. But not without assuring her pleasure before his own.

When he felt her body tighten around him, Nate knew that Jessie was close to finding her satisfaction, and sliding his hand between them, touched the tiny hidden nub of intense sensations. Her feminine muscles immediately began to gently caress him as she found her release. Only then did he give in to his own need and, tightening his arms around her, found the fulfillment of loving her.

As his strength began to return, Nate lifted her to the center of the bed, then lay down beside her. Gathering her into his arms, he reached down to pull the navy blue satin sheet over them as their bodies cooled.

Kissing the top of her head, he asked, "Are you all right, darlin'?"

"I'm wonderful," she said, snuggling into him.

"And incredible," he added. "And amazing. And—"

"I get the idea," she interrupted, laughing. "I feel the same way about you."

They were silent for a few minutes before Nate thought to ask, "Have you decided what you're going to name the baby?"

Jessie shook her head. "I thought we could do that together. Do you have a name that you're particularly fond of?"

"Not really," he admitted. He'd noticed that several of the websites he'd visited had lists of names for babies, but he hadn't even considered that she would let him help her choose a name for their daughter. "I'll start thinking about it and let you know if I come up with one I like."

"When we decide what to name her, I'd like to keep it a secret until she's born," Jessie said, hiding a yawn behind her delicate hand. "Besides not wanting people to try to talk us out of the name we choose, I want to introduce her to everyone by name."

"That works for me," he agreed. Chuckling, he asked, "I don't guess we can keep my brothers in the dark about her being a girl until then, can we?" He knew they couldn't, but if Jaron's reaction was any indication, the rest of his brothers were going to be merciless in their good-natured ribbing.

Jessie smiled tiredly and shook her head. "I promised to let your sisters-in-law know what we're having so they can choose appropriate decorations for the shower." Yawning again, her eyes drifted shut. "I'll call Bria after I get up from…our nap."

Her last couple of words were slurred and Nate knew without looking that Jessie was sound asleep. Smiling, he kissed the top of her head, arranged a pillow to support her back and eased out of bed. After a quick shower, he got dressed and, folding her discarded clothes, placed them on the bench at the end of the bed.

Heading downstairs, he walked into his office to turn on his computer. He had more research to do—this time to find names he liked for the baby.

Nate couldn't help but grin. For someone who could care less about technology, he sure had spent a lot of his time lately searching for things on the computer.

But as he read through list after list of baby names,

he found his mind wandering to the woman upstairs in his bed. How had he gotten so lucky that Jessie wanted to be with him—loved him? And there wasn't a doubt in his mind that she did. He had seen it in her eyes and felt it in her soft touch. And he'd lost count of the number of times she had said she loved something that he'd said or that it meant so much to her.

He took a deep breath and admitted to himself what he had suspected had been behind breaking up with her so many times—he had been falling for her. Every time he felt himself starting to care for Jessie more than he was comfortable with, he had cut and run in a lame attempt to avoid what he now knew had been the inevitable. He was in love with Jessie and probably had been from the moment they met.

His heart stalled and his stomach clenched almost painfully. What did he know about love?

He loved his family, but that was different. His brothers and sisters-in-law loved him and accepted him unconditionally. They weren't going to condemn him for past mistakes and the run-ins he'd had with the law when he was younger. Would Jessie be able to overlook his shortcomings and love him anyway?

Then there was his fear of reverting to the earliest example he'd had of what a husband and father was supposed to be. His biggest fear had always been that he would turn out to be like his shiftless biological father. To his knowledge Joe Rafferty had never held a job longer than it took him to show up and quit. He'd been content to spend his days sitting in front of the television with a bottle of whiskey in one hand and cigar in the other while Nate and Sam's mother worked herself to death to support all of them. After her death, Joe had abandoned his two adolescent sons to fend for themselves and went in search of another meal ticket elsewhere. They hadn't seen or heard from him again. And that was just fine with his sons. Even when the bastard was around all he had ever done was criticize and demean them.

Nate knew he wasn't anything like his old man in most ways. Unlike his father, Nate wasn't afraid to work for the things he wanted. He had put in the time and effort to get a college education, wisely invested the money that he'd earned from rodeo and amassed a sizable fortune. He had a huge ranch, a house that some might consider a mansion and enough money in the bank that he never had to work another day in his life if he didn't want to. But those were all material things. What about meeting the emotional needs of a wife and child? Could he be everything Jessie and his little girl needed him to be?

Sitting back in his desk chair, he stared at the computer screen without seeing it. Although it scared the hell out of him that he might let them down in some way, he knew he loved them and would do everything humanly possible to protect them from any kind of harm—both physical and emotional.

His biggest concern now was telling Jessie about his past and the reason he had never really considered himself husband and father material. He wasn't proud of it and would rather climb a barbed-wire fence buck naked than to have to tell her about it. But she deserved to know the truth—that the father of her baby was a convicted felon.

Could she accept being with a man who had a criminal record, even if it had been sealed by the courts because he'd been a juvenile when he committed the crimes? He was pretty sure she would understand the reasons he and Sam had resorted to breaking the law. But would she be able to trust and still love him once he laid it all on the line and told her about his childhood and the concern he had always had that he would somehow turn out to be like his worthless father? What would he do if it led her to leave him?

Nate wasn't sure. He only hoped that once he told her, she would understand and love him anyway.

Eight

When Jessie woke up from her nap, she wasn't surprised to find herself in bed alone. Nate had probably gone downstairs to his office to work on his computer. She had no idea what the project was, but it seemed that every spare minute he had, he was researching something.

Stretching, she felt a twinge in her right side and decided that she might need to invest in one of the bigger pregnancy pillows. Of course, she wouldn't need one except for naps. At night, Nate was all the support she needed.

She smiled as she got out of bed and walked into the bathroom for a quick shower. Nate had been amazing the past few weeks. He had been attentive, supportive and erased all doubt that he would be a good father. But what about her?

Her smile faded. She loved him with every fiber of her being and knew without question that she would for the rest of her life. But she wasn't sure he loved her. She knew he cared deeply for her. No man would have been as tender or as understanding of her insecurities about her pregnant body if he didn't. But he had never told her he loved her and he'd stopped mentioning that he wanted them to get married. Did that mean he had changed his mind? Could he want the baby, but not her?

She knew she could be reading more into the situation than what was there. Her hormones had been anything but stable lately and she could very well be misinterpreting things. But with no answers there was only one way to find out what was happening in their relationship. As she got dressed, she decided it was time that they sat down and had a talk about what the future held for them.

She rubbed her right side. The nagging twinge had turned to a constant dull ache. The baby was probably pressing against a nerve, she decided as she started downstairs. As active as her daughter had been lately, it felt as if she was practicing to be an Olympic gymnast.

"What do you think of Hope or Faith for the baby's name?" Nate asked, walking out of his office as she reached the bottom of the stairs.

"Hope and Faith are very nice names," she said, wondering why she suddenly felt hot and a bit weak. "Why don't we start a list of names and then choose the one we both like best?"

"It sounds like we have a plan," he said, grinning as he walked over to kiss her. Leaning back, he frowned. "Are you feeling all right? You feel pretty warm."

"I-I'm…not sure," she said haltingly when the ache in her side turned to actual pain.

"Jessie, what's wrong?" he demanded, holding her up when her knees started to buckle.

"Nate…something's…wrong," she said, holding on to the front of his shirt when another wave of weakness washed over her.

He quickly swept her up into his arms and instead of climbing the stairs, hurried to place her on the couch in the family room. "I'm calling Life Flight," he said, taking his cell phone from the holder on his belt.

While Nate made the call to the emergency service, Jessie's nurse's training kicked in and, assessing her symptoms, she was fairly certain she had a hot appendix. If that was the case, she was going to need surgery. That was a significant risk to the baby and she wanted the best care possible.

"Tell them I'm twenty-one weeks pregnant and showing symptoms of appendicitis," she instructed, trying to keep her growing panic at bay. "I need to go to the hospital where I work. It's a Level 1 Trauma Center and they'll be better able to deal with whatever I need to have done."

After giving the air-ambulance service the information and their location, Nate knelt down beside her and held her hand. "Stephenville Hospital is closer, darlin'. We could see a doctor sooner if you go there."

She shook her head. "If I have to have surgery it

might cause me…to go into labor," she tried to explain. Breathless from the pain, she finished, "The hospital where I work has one of the…best neonatology units… in the state. It's where our baby would have…the best chance of survival if she's born because of this."

"I give you my word that's where I'll make them take you," he stated.

Jessie could tell by the determined look on Nate's handsome face that if the paramedics tried to talk him into letting them take her to the nearest hospital in Stephenville, they would have a fight on their hands. And although that was normal medical protocol, she knew what she needed and didn't want to waste the time being assessed by the medical staff in Stephenville only to be sent to Waco later anyway. That would be a huge waste of precious time and might prove to be too late for her or the baby—or both.

As soon as the helicopter took off with Jessie on board, Nate jumped into his truck and drove like a bat out of hell toward Waco. When he asked if he could go with them, he was told there wasn't enough room. Although he hated being away from her, he understood. He wanted them to be able to do whatever needed to be done for Jessie and if that meant leaving him to get to the hospital on his own, then so be it. Fortunately, he had a friend who was a member of the Texas Highway Patrol and with one phone call to explain the situation and what he needed, Nate had a police escort from Beaver Dam all the way to the hospital's parking lot.

Even though he made the drive in record time, when

he ran into the hospital and up to the desk in the ER, he felt like it had been an eternity since he had watched the helicopter lift off from his ranch yard. "My...wife, Jessica Farrell was brought in a little while ago by helicopter," he informed the older woman behind the desk. "She's five and a half months pregnant and thinks she might have appendicitis."

The woman nodded. "She's in triage now and the trauma surgeon on call is with her. If you'll please have a seat in the waiting area, the doctor will come out and talk to you as soon as he's finished assessing your wife."

Too keyed up to sit still, Nate stepped outside to make a quick call to his brother Sam to let the family know what was going on, then went back inside to stand just outside the double doors leading back to the examination rooms. He had lied to the receptionist about being married to Jessie, but he didn't give a damn. Jessie was his woman, pregnant with his baby and he didn't want to take the chance of them refusing to give him any information about her condition or allowing him to see her.

"Sir, I'm afraid you'll have to go to the waiting room," the older woman insisted when she noticed him stationed by the doors.

Walking back to the desk where she sat, he shook his head. "Ma'am, I'm sorry, but I can't do that. My whole world is just beyond those doors and if I can't be with her, then I want to be as close to her as I can get."

The woman stared at him for a moment before she pointed to a spot close to where he had been standing.

"Stand over there, son. You'll be out of the way and as close as I can let you get right now." She gave him a reassuring smile. "I'm sure the doctor will be out soon to tell you what her diagnosis is and what they need to do to treat her."

"Thank you," Nate said, walking over to where the woman had indicated.

He could see through the small narrow windows on the doors, but he had no idea where Jessie was and his view was obscured by the drawn curtains of the cubicles. Glancing at the clock on the wall, he wondered what the hell could be taking so long. They needed to do something and soon.

Nate's stomach drew up into a tight knot when he watched a man in blue scrubs and a white lab coat leave one of the cubicles and start walking toward the doors. Opening one of them, he asked, "Mr. Farrell?"

"The name's Rafferty," Nate said. "Jessica Farrell is my wife." That was twice he'd lied in the past twenty minutes and two times more than he had in the past twenty years. But he wasn't taking any chances of them not letting him know what was going on.

He briefly thought the doctor might question them having different last names. But the man didn't even bat an eye. Of course, a lot of married women chose to keep their own surnames these days, so he probably didn't think there was anything unusual about it.

"I'm Dr. Chavez," he introduced himself. "I'm the trauma surgeon who will be doing your wife's appendectomy. She was right about having appendicitis and we need to get her into surgery right away to keep the appendix from rupturing. Under normal circumstances it would be a routine surgery. But because of her pregnancy it raises the risk to both her and the fetus. I've called in a team of specialists to stand by in case the surgery throws your wife into labor and we have to take the baby by C-section."

"Can I see her before the surgery?" Nate asked, needing to let her know he was there for her. If they'd let him, he'd go into surgery with her. He knew they wouldn't allow that, but he would gladly go if he could.

The doctor motioned for Nate to follow him. "Some of the surgical team will be coming anytime to take her upstairs to surgery and we've already administered a preop sedative, so I doubt you'll be able to talk to her." He stopped Nate just outside the curtained-off cubicle. "I want to assure you that we'll do everything we can for both her and the baby, Mr. Rafferty. But as I said before, there are risks for both of them."

Nate felt as if his entire world was falling apart around him. With a lump the size of his fist clogging his throat, he did his best to clear it and get the words out that no man ever wanted to have to say. "If it comes down to saving her or the baby, please save Jessie."

Dr. Chavez nodded. "We'll do all we can."

While the doctor hurried off to scrub for surgery, Nate stepped into the cubicle and walked up to the bed where Jessie lay with her eyes closed. Taking her hand in his, he gave it a gentle squeeze. "Jessie, I'm here for you now and always will be, darlin'," he said, feeling about as helpless as he could ever remember.

What had kept him from telling her he loved her

when deep down he was sure that's all she'd ever wanted from him? Why had he waited, instead of truly giving her his all? Jessie deserved to know everything about him and he wanted nothing more than to tell her and beg her to love him in spite of it. But had he waited too long? Dear God, would he even have another chance?

Before he could tell her how much he loved her and needed her more than the air he breathed, two members of the surgical team opened the curtain. "We're going to take your wife upstairs now, Mr. Rafferty," one of them said. "You can go up to the surgical waiting room on the fourth floor. The doctor will see you up there after the surgery is over to let you know how everything went."

Nate leaned over the rail to kiss Jessie's forehead and reluctantly let go of her hand as the two nurses moved the bed out into the hall. As he stood there watching them roll her away from him, he would have given anything to trade places with her—to go through this crisis so she didn't have to. When they moved the bed through a set of doors at the end of the hall and out of his sight, Nate took several shuddering breaths. Feeling a drop of moisture on his cheek, he impatiently swiped it away and headed for the elevators. He hadn't cried since he was fifteen years old, but he found himself fighting with everything he had in him to keep his emotions in check as he rode the elevator alone to the fourth floor, got off and walked into the waiting area.

Finding a corner of the big room that was relatively deserted, he sat down and stared at his boot tops. There weren't a lot of things he was afraid of. He could climb on the back of one of the biggest, rankest bulls, get thrown off and stare death in the face when the ornery animal came after him and never think a thing about it. But right now he was scared to death.

What if he lost Jessie? Or what if something happened to the baby? They hadn't even had the chance to give their little girl a name.

Scrubbing his palms over his face to push away the emotion threatening to swamp him, he leaned forward to rest his forearms on his knees and stare down at his loosely clasped hands. Hank had always told him and his brothers that a positive attitude was half of any battle. But it was damned hard to have positive thoughts when all of the what-ifs were bombarding him from all sides.

"Have you heard anything, Nate?"

At the sound of Sam's voice, Nate looked up to see all five of his brothers walking across the waiting room toward him. He wasn't the least bit surprised that they had all dropped whatever they were doing to come to the hospital to lend their moral support. It had been that way for the six of them since their days at the Last Chance Ranch. They had each other's back no matter what and he'd never been more glad to see them than he was at that moment.

"They took her into surgery about an hour ago," he said, glancing at the clock over the waiting room doors.

"What did the doctor say?" Ryder asked, sitting down beside him.

Explaining what had taken place and the doctor's

diagnosis, Nate finished, "He has a team of specialists standing by in case something happens and they have to deliver the baby."

"Everything is going to work out, Nate," T.J. insisted. "Jessie and the baby are both going to come through this with flying colors."

The most optimistic of the band of brothers, T.J. was always the one they could count on to lift their spirits when they were down. But as much as Nate tried to believe his brother, he couldn't stop thinking about the look on the doctor's face when Chavez told him about the risks to Jessie's and the baby's lives.

"T.J.'s right," Sam said, nodding. He sat down in the chair across from Nate. "Jessie and the baby will both be fine. You have to believe that."

Nodding, Nate took a deep breath. "We just found out a few days ago that we're having a girl."

Giving him a reassuring smile, Ryder placed his hand on Nate's shoulders. "About sixteen years from now, when our girls start dating, we can trade what scare tactics we're using to keep the boys in line."

"The day of the ultrasound I decided it might not be a bad idea to get a couple more guns to clean," Nate said, praying that he had reason to do just that.

"T.J., why don't you and I run down to the cafeteria to get us all a cup of coffee," Lane suggested.

"Good idea," T.J. said, nodding. "Hang in there, Nate. We'll be right back."

Nate nodded as he watched them leave. The last time he sat in a hospital waiting room it was with Bria when they were waiting on word about Sam's concussion. That had been two and half years ago—the day he met Jessie.

While Ryder and Sam started talking about Bria and Summer getting babysitters so they could join the men at the hospital, Jaron lowered himself into the chair on the other side of Nate. He had always been the quiet one of the bunch, but he was more silent than usual.

"What's up, bro?" Nate asked, careful to keep his voice low.

Jaron shrugged. "I was just wondering if anyone thought to call Mariah and let her know what happened. You know how she gets her nose out of joint when something's going on with the family and she doesn't know about it."

Nate shook his head. "I'm not sure. Maybe you better give her a call and tell her."

Nate knew that Jaron was looking for an excuse to talk to Mariah and he couldn't help but wonder how much longer his brother was going to be able to resist what the rest of them had known for years. Jaron and Mariah were meant to be together.

Jaron hesitated for a minute before he stood up. "I probably better go outside for that. You know how the staff gets when somebody uses a cell phone inside the hospital."

Nate didn't bother pointing out that most hospitals had relaxed their rules about cell phone use. Jaron was trying to avoid the rest of their brothers ribbing him later about calling her.

When Jaron walked out of the room to make his call to Mariah, Lane and T.J. returned with the coffee and handed one of the cups to Jaron as they passed in the doorway. Nate watched them talk for a moment before Lane and T.J. continued across the room.

Accepting the cup Lane handed him and unable to sit still any longer, Nate stood up and walked over to the window overlooking the street below. What could be taking so long? It had been almost two hours since they took Jessie into surgery and every damn minute of it had been pure hell for him.

"You okay?" Sam asked, walking over to join him.

Nate gave a short nod. "I just couldn't sit still anymore. I feel like I need to be doing something, but there isn't a damned thing I can do to protect her and the baby from this."

"I understand." His brother hooked his thumb toward the door. "Do you need to go outside for some air?"

"No, I'm not leaving," Nate said firmly. He took a sip of the bitter coffee. "As far as that goes, I don't intend to leave until I take Jessie home with me."

Sam nodded. "I'd feel the same way if Bria was the one in the operating room."

The sound of his brothers rising to their feet to join him and Sam by the window in a gesture of support had Nate turning to see Dr. Chavez making his way over to him. Whether from dread of what the man might say, relief that the surgery was over or the emotion threatening his composure, Nate couldn't for the life of him find his voice to ask the man if Jessie was all right.

"Mr. Rafferty, your wife made it through the surgery with no problems," he said, reaching up to remove his surgical cap. "We were lucky and got the appendix out before it ruptured. Everything is fine and she should be able to go home in a couple of days."

"Thank God!" The relief flowing through Nate was so intense it caused him to feel a little light-headed. "What about the baby?"

"We're good there as well," the doctor said, smiling for the first time since Nate met him in the ER. "I had an ob-gyn who specializes in high-risk pregnancies monitor the fetus throughout the surgery and she'll continue to watch things while Jessie is in recovery."

"When can I see her?" Nate needed to see for himself that Jessie was all right.

Dr. Chavez checked his watch. "They should be moving her to a room in about an hour. You'll be able to see her then, but I doubt you'll be able to talk to her much. The remnants of the anesthesia are going to cause her to sleep and she probably won't be completely out from under that until morning."

For the first time since Jessie came downstairs after her nap that afternoon, Nate felt some of the gut-wrenching fear that had held him in its grip begin to ease. "I can't thank you enough, doc," Nate said, shaking the man's hand. As the doctor turned to leave, Nate suddenly felt like his knees might buckle and, making it over to one of the chairs, he sat down.

"What's this about 'your wife'?" Ryder asked, raising one dark eyebrow. "Do you have something you'd like to tell us, bro?"

Nate shook his head. "I lied and told them Jessie was my wife. Hank might be spinning in his grave right about now because one of his boys wasn't completely honest, but I didn't want to take a chance that they wouldn't let me see her or let me know what was happening."

"If we'd been in your shoes, any one of us would have done the same thing," Lane stated. All of his brothers nodded in unison.

"How's that going for you?" T.J. asked. "Any progress toward changing her mind about getting married?"

"To tell you the truth, we haven't got around to talking about it lately," Nate admitted. "But that's going to change as soon as she gets out of the hospital and I take her home. I don't care if I have to wear out the knees on a new pair of jeans from begging. I'm going to do whatever it takes to make Jessie my wife."

Nine

When Jessie roused the room was dark and for a brief moment she wondered where she was and why the right side of her stomach was extremely sore. Looking around, she realized she was in a hospital room and vaguely remembered being airlifted from Nate's ranch to the hospital where she worked because she had appendicitis.

Suddenly frightened by what that could mean, she immediately placed her hand on her stomach. "My baby," she whispered.

As if responding to her mother's voice, Jessie's little girl moved, then gave her a definite poke. Tears of joy filled Jessie's eyes and her breath caught on a sob. Her baby was all right.

Saying a silent prayer of thanks, she became aware

of another person in the room and turning her head she found Nate sitting in a chair beside the bed. With his head leaned back at an odd angle, his arms folded across his chest and his long legs extended out in front of him and crossed at the ankles, she could tell he was sound asleep. He looked uncomfortable and she started to wake him, but her eyelids were so heavy and, unable to stop herself, she let them drift shut.

Sometime before dawn, a lab worker woke Jessie to draw blood for testing and she noticed that the chair beside her hospital bed was empty. Where was Nate? Why hadn't he stayed with her? For a brief moment she thought she heard his voice as the lab worker left the room, but the shadows began to close in on her and she once again fell back to sleep.

"It's time to wake up and eat your breakfast, darlin'."

At the sound of Nate's deep baritone, Jessie opened her eyes and for the first time since she was given a preop sedative in the ER she didn't feel like she was struggling to get through a thick fog. "Were you here all night?" she asked, knowing by the shadow of beard on his lean cheeks that he had been.

"I wouldn't think of being anywhere else." He pointed to the tray of food on the overbed table. "The nurse told me I could raise the head of the bed so you can eat."

She eyed the bowl of Cream of Wheat. Just the sight of it caused her to shudder. "I'm not all that hungry. But I will eat the yogurt and drink the milk."

"Not a fan of the cereal?" he asked, pushing the

button on the side of the bed to raise it until she was a little more upright.

"No." When he took the foil top off the yogurt and handed it to her along with a spoon, she asked, "Did they say when I'll be discharged?"

"I talked to the hospitalist just a little while ago and he said you might be going home as early as tomorrow morning." He shook his head. "They sure don't keep patients in the hospital as long as they used to."

She ate most of the yogurt, then took a drink of the milk. "How did you get them to let you stay here in the room with me last night? Hospital policy discourages after-hours visitors."

He shrugged. "I refused to leave."

"And they didn't call security?" she asked, unable to believe he'd gotten away with it.

"They did, but I knew the guard." Grinning, he took the empty yogurt carton and spoon from her. "For the past couple of years he's been one of the Justin Heelers attending to injuries during the annual rodeo my brothers and I put on in honor of our foster dad. He convinced the nurses that I'm relatively harmless."

Moving the overbed table out of the way, he lowered the rail on the bed and sat on the edge of the mattress beside her. "I need to tell you something."

"What is it?" she asked. "Is it the baby? I think I remember feeling her move sometime during the night. She's okay, isn't she?"

"Everything is fine with the baby," he reassured her. "It's something I did yesterday when I first arrived at the hospital that you might not like too much."

Relieved that the baby was indeed all right, she breathed a little easier. "What did you do?"

He gave her a sheepish grin. "Don't be surprised if the nurses and doctor refer to me as your husband."

"Why?" She couldn't imagine why he would do that.

Taking her hands in his, he explained, "They had already given you a sedative and I wasn't sure they'd let me in the room to see you before they took you into surgery or give me any kind of information about your condition if I didn't tell them you were my wife."

As she thought about it, she had to admit he had a point. Privacy was a big issue and he might very well have been denied visitation as well as information.

"Okay, I won't correct them," she promised. "But when we get back to your place, we need to talk about some things."

He nodded. "I've been thinking the same thing, darlin'." His expression turned as serious as she had ever seen. "I'd talk to you here, but I want privacy for some of the things I have to tell you."

"All right," she agreed, wondering what he was going to say.

When he leaned forward, he gave her a gentle kiss. "If you don't mind, I think I'm going to go home for a shower and to change clothes. Is there anything you need me to bring to you this afternoon when I return?"

"I'll need some clothes to wear back to your place tomorrow." They had cut her clothes off her in the ER and she wasn't about to go back to his ranch in a hospital gown. "There's a denim dress in the closet that would be perfect." The elastic waistband on her maternity slacks might put pressure on her incision and she wanted to avoid the irritation if possible.

"Anything else?" he asked. "Do you want me to get in touch with your folks and let them know what happened?"

Jessie shook her head. "I'll call them after we go back to your place."

It wasn't like they would have taken the time away from their real estate business to make the drive up from Houston to see about her anyway. She'd have to explain her relationship with her parents and why Nate had never met them. But that could wait until they returned to Nate's ranch. She was more curious about what Nate had to tell her that he wanted kept private.

When Nate pulled the Mercedes he rarely drove into the garage, Jessie waited until he came around to help her out of the car. He knew she was sore and moving slower than normal, but it was good to have her back at the Twin Oaks Ranch. Working at a hospital was one thing, but being a patient there was another matter entirely and he knew she was glad to leave. The two times he had to be hospitalized because of a rodeo injury, he had come to understand why so many people complained about needing to go home just to get some rest. It seemed that every hour someone came into the room to draw blood or take vital signs. And just as sure as he went to sleep, a nurse would wake him up to ask if he needed something.

"I'm so glad to be back here," Jessie commented as he helped her into the house.

"I had Rosemary make up the downstairs guest room because I thought steps might not be a good idea this soon after surgery," he said as they walked down the hall.

"That's probably a good idea." She smiled. "As slow as I'm moving it would probably take all night just to get up the stairs."

"Would you like to change into one of your nightshirts and lie down for a while?" Nate asked, wondering if she was tired from the hour's drive.

"No, I've been in bed for the past two days and I'd really like to be up for a while," she said, turning toward the family room.

"Do you want something to eat or drink?" he asked, trying to think if there was something else she might need.

She smiled. "You aren't going to hover, are you?"

"I'm just trying to make sure you're comfortable." He frowned. "Why do you ask?"

"Summer and Bria stopped by the hospital yesterday afternoon and they were telling me about Ryder's propensity to hover over Summer whenever she's ill," Jessie said, grinning. "I just wondered if you were going to be like him."

"Yeah, he does have a tendency to be an old mother hen where Summer and little Katie are concerned." Nate was beginning to understand how his brother felt about taking care of the woman and child he loved more than life itself. "Is there anything else you need?"

"Yes," she said as she sat down on the couch. "I'd

like to have that talk we discussed in the hospital yesterday."

What he had to tell her was going to take some time and was without question the most important conversation of his entire life, not to mention the most difficult. He was going to be laying his soul bare to her and once started it wasn't something that could be interrupted and picked up later. He could only hope she understood and loved him anyway.

"Are you sure you're up to it?" he asked.

She stared at him for a moment before she nodded. "Whether I'm going to like hearing what you want to tell me or not, things can't go on between us the way they've been, Nate."

"I agree," he said, praying she would understand and forgive him. Deciding there was no easy way to tell her about his past, he took a deep breath. "I'm a convicted felon."

Nate could tell by her shocked expression that was the last thing she expected. "When did that happen?"

"I told you up front that my brothers and I were foster kids and met when we all ended up being sent to the Last Chance Ranch," he said, reaching up to rub the growing tension at the back of his neck. "Believe me, we weren't sent there because we were little angels."

"I always assumed it was just a name," she said, shaking her head. "I didn't realize it had a literal meaning."

"Yeah, it was our last shot at keeping ourselves from being incarcerated," he stated flatly. "It was either finish growing up there or behind bars in a juvenile detention facility."

"What did you do that you were arrested?" she asked, her tone quiet.

"Sam and I started out stealing food and then graduated to robbing stores at gunpoint for cash." Unable to look at her for fear of seeing the condemnation on her pretty face, he walked over to gaze out the window at the land that represented how far he'd come in life.

She frowned. "What caused you to start stealing food?"

He shrugged. "Why does any kid start shoplifting food? We were hungry."

"Didn't your previous foster parents see that you had enough to eat?" He appreciated the indignation in her voice, but she had it wrong.

"Darlin', we didn't land in foster care until after we got caught robbing a convenience store," he admitted. "That was after our mom passed away and our dad abandoned us."

She gasped. "Oh, Nate, I'm so sorry."

"Don't be. The day our dad walked out and disappeared for good was the luckiest day of our lives," Nate said, unable to keep the bitterness from his voice. "He sat on his ass and let our mom work herself to death to support the four of us because he was too lazy to keep a job. And that wasn't his only flaw. He liked making us feel like it was our fault for everything that went wrong in his life. He had a way of talking to us that undermined any self-esteem or confidence we had."

"He was abusive?" she asked, sounding angry.

"Not physically. That would have required him to set down the bottle of whiskey he was nursing and get out of his recliner." Turning to face her, he shook his head. "Joe Rafferty preferred the mental abuse of telling us how worthless and pathetic we were."

"It sounds like it *was* the luckiest day of your lives," Jessie agreed. "How old were you when he left?"

"I was thirteen and Sam was fifteen when he cut out for good," Nate admitted. "We had been shoplifting food for a year or so, but it wasn't until he left that we found a gun he left behind in the hall closet. That's when we started holding up stores at gunpoint for the cash." He shook his head as he turned back to the window. "We had the idea that if we kept the bills paid, we'd be able to stay in the house and not end up sleeping in a back alley somewhere or put into the foster care system."

"How long were you able to keep up the ruse that you and Sam weren't on your own?" she asked, frowning. "I wouldn't think it would be all that easy."

"I can't remember exactly, but it wasn't too long," he admitted. "Probably a few months."

"How did you get caught?" He detected sympathy in her voice that he neither wanted nor deserved.

Looking back he couldn't believe how naive he'd been. "Sam was gone somewhere and I decided to hit a convenience store by myself because a final notice for the rent was posted on the door when I got home from school. I thought I would get the money we needed and everything would be fine."

"You continued to go to school?" She sounded surprised. "Most children wouldn't have tried to continue their education."

"We thought that if we kept going to school and made sure all the bills got paid, no one would be the wiser about the old man leaving and we would avoid being separated in the foster-care system." He shook his head. "I honestly don't know how we figured we would get away with it, but we tried."

"Children don't think things through like adults," Jessie said softly.

Nate walked over to sit on the coffee table in front of her. "That was apparent when Sam tried to take the blame and keep me out of trouble." He shook his head. "We didn't know it, but the police had been watching us and suspected we were the pair of kids robbing the stores around our neighborhood."

"You were only trying to survive and stay together," she said, reaching out to place her hand on his arm. "You were all the other had."

"That didn't make what we did right," he insisted. He needed her to understand that he wasn't telling her about his past to garner her sympathy. He was trying to explain why he had avoided making commitments and his fear of turning out to be like his father. "The bottom line is that I broke the law and even though the court records were sealed because we were underage, I'm still a convicted felon." He took a deep breath. "The main reason I kept breaking off our relationship when things started getting too serious was the fear I have that I would somehow turn out to be like our worthless old man."

She looked confused. "I'm afraid I don't see what that has to do with—"

"Until our dad took off and left me and Sam to fend for ourselves, all I heard was how useless I was. Then when I got in trouble and ended up with a record, I started to believe I was going to turn out just like the son of bitch who sired me." He took both of her hands in his. "All of my adult life, I've run from making a commitment because I didn't want to saddle a woman with a man like that. I didn't want my kids to suffer that kind of mental abuse. I don't intend to be that kind of man, but there are no guarantees, darlin'. All I can do is promise that I'll do everything in my power to be the best husband and father I can be."

"But you're nothing like your father," she insisted. She reached up to cup his cheek with her palm, sending hope coursing through him. "You're a good man, Nate. You've worked hard and earned everything you have. It sounds to me like that's something your father would have never thought of doing."

"I'm still a criminal," he said, wishing he could go back in time and change that part of his life. "You deserve better than that, Jessie."

"Stop it right now!" she said forcefully. "You had problems as a boy and a misguided belief that you could somehow make it all right. But you learned from your mistakes and thanks to Hank Calvert and his unique approach to teaching you right from wrong, you and your brothers have all turned your lives around. Any woman would be proud to call you her man."

"What about you, Jessie?" he asked. "Would you be

proud to call me your man?" He held his breath as he waited for her answer.

When she continued to stare at him, his heart felt like it had stopped beating. "What are you saying, Nate?" she finally asked.

He was pretty sure he knew what she wanted from him and for the first time in his life, he was ready to say it. "I love you, Jessie. Do you think you can overlook what I was before and be proud to be with the man I am now?"

Tears flooded her eyes and rolled down her cheeks. "Y-yes, Nate. All I've ever wanted is for you to love me."

Nate immediately dropped to one knee and, reaching into his front jeans pocket, removed the small black velvet box he'd been carrying around since stopping by the jewelers on his way back to the hospital yesterday afternoon. Taking her hand in his, he asked, "Will you marry me, Jessie? Will you let me make you proud to call me your husband for the rest of our lives?"

"Yes," she whispered. "I love you so much. I've always loved you."

He took the two-carat marquise-shaped diamond ring from the box and slipped it on the third finger of her left hand. When she started to lean forward to put her arms around his neck, he stopped her. "You just had surgery," he said, scooping her up in his arms. He sat down on the couch and gently placed her on his lap. "I don't want you hurting yourself."

Content to have her in his arms, they were silent for

a few minutes before he asked, "When do you want to get married, darlin'?"

She kissed him. "I know you have the National Finals the first part of December—"

"Do you think you'll be able to watch me make my last rides in Vegas?" he asked.

"You're going to stop riding?" she asked, looking hopeful.

He nodded. "Part of my job as your husband will be to eliminate as much of your stress and worry as I possibly can."

"I don't want you giving up your career because of my fears," she said, frowning.

"I'm not." He kissed the tip of her nose. "Jaron and I have both talked about retiring while we're still on top."

"Are you sure?"

"Positive."

"I'm not going to say that I won't resume my nursing career at some point in time, but I think I'd like to be a stay-at-home mom," she said thoughtfully. "At least, until our daughter starts school."

"Whatever you want to do is fine with me, darlin'." He held her close. "Now when do you want to get married?"

"Is Christmas too soon?" she asked, snuggling against him.

"Hell, no." He laughed. "The sooner the better."

"Are you going to ask Sam to be your best man?" Jessie asked, her smile radiant.

"Yeah, he's been my partner in crime all my life,"

Nate said, grinning. "I don't see any reason to change that now."

Jessie rolled her eyes. "You're impossible." Kissing him again, she smiled. "I thought I would ask Bria to be my matron of honor."

"Well, now that we have the wedding planned, we can move up the date," he teased. He'd never felt happier or more lighthearted in his entire life. "Darlin', you mentioned earlier that you had something you wanted to talk to me about. What was it?"

He watched her worry her lower lip for a moment before she admitted, "Just before I had the appendicitis attack, I was going to ask you if you had changed your mind about wanting us to get married."

"Why would you think that?" he asked, holding her close.

She laughed and it was the most delightful sound he'd ever heard. "You hadn't mentioned it and I thought you had lost interest in our relationship again."

"I made you a promise," he said, tipping her chin up to give her a kiss that rocked him to his core. "I gave you my word I wouldn't pressure you about getting married. And believe me, that wasn't easy when it was just about all I could think of."

"You could have hinted at it," she said, smiling.

"That would have broken my promise to you and that's something I will never do," he said honestly.

She stared at him a moment before she spoke again. "I have a confession to make."

"What's that, darlin'?" he asked, wondering what her secret could possibly be.

"You aren't the only one who has a parent they aren't particularly happy with," she admitted. "I have two that could improve in a lot of areas."

Nate listened to her explain about her parents having more interest in someone's net worth than the person. "I didn't want you having to go through the third degree about your bank account when it's none of their business," she finished.

Grinning, he whispered a number in her ear. "Do you think that would impress them?"

Her eyes were wide when she nodded. "Is that…"

"What I was worth a couple of years ago." He laughed. "My investment banker says I have a lot more now."

"I knew you spent a lot of time on the internet, but I had no idea you were watching the stock market," she said, shaking her head.

"Hell, I don't pay attention to the market," he said, laughing. "That stuff will make you crazy in a hurry."

"Then what were you researching if not stocks to invest in?" she asked, clearly confused.

"I wanted to learn all I could about pregnancy and what you were going through." He gave her a sheepish grin. "I was looking to see how I could make the next few months easier for you." He placed his hand on her stomach. "And I wanted to find out what was going on with our little girl."

When he felt the light movement within, his heart stalled. "Wow! She's moving, isn't she?"

Jessie nodded. "She's really active and I think she might be training to be a gymnast."

Nate knew he had to be grinning like a damned fool. "Thank you, Jessie."

"For what?" she asked, looking puzzled.

"You've given me everything I didn't even know I wanted," he said, kissing her with all the love he'd never dreamed would be his.

When he stared into her pretty violet eyes, he could see his haven—his safe place to land when life got to be more than he could handle on his own. And he fully intended to be the same for her.

"I love you, darlin'," he said, never wanting her to doubt it. "You and the baby are my world."

"And you're ours, cowboy," she said, pressing her soft, perfect lips to his. "Now and always."

Epilogue

On Christmas Eve as Nate waited by the fireplace in the Twin Oaks ranch house with Sam and the preacher from the church in Beaver Dam, he checked his watch. Within the next ten minutes or so, Jessie would be his wife and he was getting impatient. It seemed as though he had already spent a lifetime waiting for her. He couldn't wait to get started on the rest of his life with her.

"You aren't getting cold feet, are you?" Sam asked when Nate checked his watch again.

"No, I'd like to seal the deal before she changes *her* mind," Nate answered.

His brother laughed. "I never thought I'd see the day you'd be impatient to settle down."

"Yeah, it shocked the hell out of me, too," Nate said, grinning.

When the organist he had hired to play for the wedding broke into the first few notes of "Here Comes the Bride," Nate straightened his shoulders and looked toward the double doorway leading from the foyer into the family room. As he watched his sister-in-law Bria start to walk toward them, he held his breath and waited for Jessie and her father to step into view.

When he and Jessie went down to Houston right after Thanksgiving to tell the Farrells they were about to gain a soon-to-be retired rodeo cowboy for a son-in-law over Christmas and become the grandparents of a granddaughter in the spring, they had been anything but happy. But when Nate took Andrew Farrell aside and assured him that he loved Jessie, told him there wouldn't be a prenuptial agreement and had the man call Nate's investment banker to verify that Nate had more than enough to pay cash for any of the overpriced properties their real estate agency represented, they couldn't have been more enthusiastic. Nate didn't give a damn what they thought of him or how welcoming they were. All he wanted from them was a change in the way they treated Jessie, even if it did hinge on his, and now their daughter's, net worth. He loved her more than enough to make up for their shallow affections and that was something that would never come with a price tag attached.

The moment Jessie and her dad came into view and he saw her beautiful face, Nate's heart beat double time. She was absolutely gorgeous in her long white wedding gown and he knew for certain he would re-member the moment for the rest of his days. He still had a hard time believing that in just a few minutes she would be his forever.

Waiting impatiently for them to reach him, when her father placed her hand in his, Nate felt as though he had been handed a rare and precious gift. "Are you ready to become Mrs. Nate Rafferty?" he asked, smiling at the only woman he would ever love.

Her smile lit his soul when she whispered, "I've been ready for this my entire life."

"Welcome to the ranks of the blissfully hitched," Ryder said, raising his beer bottle to toast Nate.

"I didn't think I'd ever say this, but I couldn't be happier about becoming a member of the club," Nate said, meaning it.

"Yeah, membership is damned nice," T.J. said, grinning as he looked over at his wife. They had announced at Thanksgiving that they were expecting to add another family member sometime in the summer and from what Heather told Jessie, T.J. had started hovering over her like Ryder did over his wife, Summer.

"So who won the pool?" Nate asked, taking a swig of his beer. "Didn't T.J. say we would be married by Christmas?"

Lane nodded. "I think he's won a couple of our betting pools lately."

"So what are we going to bet on now?" Sam asked.

Their gazes all swung toward Jaron.

"Oh, *hell* no," Jaron said, shaking his head vehemently. "I'm just fine on my own."

"I say Jaron and Mariah will be hitched by next fall," T.J. said, plunking down a hundred dollars on the bar.

"I've got Easter," Ryder spoke up, putting a hundred on top of T.J.'s.

"I'm going with Valentine's Day," Lane said, adding his money to the growing pile of bills.

"I've got the 4th of July." Sam added his bet. "What about you, Nate?"

"I'll take May," Nate said, topping off the pile of money with his hundred. He looked at his best friend, who was quietly fuming at being the subject of the betting frenzy. "Sorry, bro. But I have to agree with the others. Whenever you and Mariah are within twenty feet of each other, you could cut the tension with a knife."

"Probably because she wants to tear my head off and shout down the hole," Jaron shot back. "She still hasn't gotten over me being right about Sam and Lane both having boys when Bria and Taylor got pregnant."

"But she was right about me and Summer having a girl," Ryder interjected. "That should have made her happy."

"It did, right up until Lane and Taylor had a boy," Jaron said, shaking his head. "She took exception to me pointing out that I'd called it right two thirds of the time and she had only been right once."

"Yeah, women take a dim view of a man making comments like that," Sam said, laughing.

As the brothers continued to try to convince Jaron

that he and Mariah were destined to be together, Nate looked up to see Jessie smiling at him. It was the same smile she wore the night he had won the bull riding event at the National Finals rodeo—the night he had announced his retirement. Setting his beer bottle on the bar, he walked across the dance floor to take her in his arms.

"As nice as this reception is, I'm ready to start the honeymoon," he whispered. "How about you, Mrs. Rafferty?"

She nodded. "I love everyone and I couldn't be happier about becoming a member of the family, but I'd like to spend some time alone with my new husband."

Nate nodded toward her parents. "Do you think they'll be all right on their own?"

Jessie rolled her eyes. "Don't worry about them. I saw my dad pass out a couple of business cards to some of your rodeo friends."

He laughed. "Yeah, he never dreamed that rodeo cowboys could make damned good money riding a dusty old bull."

"Not until the most handsome retired cowboy I know enlightened him," she said, raising up on tiptoe to kiss his chin.

When the baby landed a kick to his navel, Nate chuckled. "I think she agrees with you."

"I think so," Jessie said, her beautiful smile sending his blood pressure sky high.

"Let's go get started on our life together," he said, taking her hand to lead her toward the door.

"I love you, cowboy," she said, looking up at him with more love in her eyes than he would ever deserve.

"And I love you, darlin'," he said, feeling like the luckiest man alive. "Forever and always."

* * * * *

THE GOOD, THE BAD AND THE TEXAN:
*Running with these billionaires
will be one wild ride.
Don't miss a single novel in this
bestselling series from*
USA TODAY *bestselling author Kathie DeNosky!*

*HIS MARRIAGE TO REMEMBER
A BABY BETWEEN FRIENDS
YOUR RANCH...OR MINE?
THE COWBOY'S WAY
PREGNANT WITH THE RANCHER'S BABY*

All available now, only from Harlequin Desire!

*If you're on Twitter, tell us what you think
of Harlequin Desire! #harlequindesire*

RECLAIMED BY
THE RANCHER
Janice Maynard

One

Not much rattled Jeff Hartley. At twenty-nine, he owned and operated the family ranch where he had grown up during a near-idyllic childhood. His parents had taken early retirement back in the spring and had headed off to a condo on Galveston Bay, leaving their only son to carry on the tradition.

Jeff was a full member of the prestigious Texas Cattleman's Club, a venerable establishment where the movers and shakers of Royal, Texas, met to shoot the breeze and oftentimes conduct business. Jeff prided himself on being mature, efficient, easygoing and practical.

But when he opened his door on a warm October afternoon and saw Lucy Peyton standing on his front porch, it felt as if a bull had kicked him in the chest.

First there was the dearth of oxygen, a damned scary feeling. Then the pain set in. After that, he had the impulse to flee before the bull could take another shot.

He stared at his visitor, his gaze as level and dispassionate as he could make it. "I plan to vote Democrat this year. I don't need any magazine subscriptions. And I already have a church home," he said. "But thanks for stopping by."

He almost had the door closed before she spoke. "Jeff. Please. I need to talk to you."

Damn it. How could a woman say his name—one measly syllable—and make his insides go all wonky? Her voice was every bit the same as he remembered. Soft and husky…as if she were on the verge of laryngitis. Or perhaps about to offer some lucky man naughty, unspeakable pleasure in the bedroom.

The sound of eight words, no matter how urgently spoken, shouldn't have made him weak in the knees.

Her looks hadn't changed, either, though she was a bit thinner than he remembered. Her dark brown hair, all one length but parted on the side, brushed her shoulders. Hazel eyes still reminded him of an autumn pond filled with fallen leaves.

She was tall, at least five-eight…and though she was athletic and graceful, she had plenty of curves to add interest to the map. Some of those curves still kept him awake on dark, troubled nights.

"Unless you're here to apologize," he said, his words deliberately curt, "I don't think we have anything to talk about."

When she shoved her shoulder against the door, he

had to step back or risk hurting her. Even so, he planted himself in the doorway, drawing a metaphorical line in the sand.

Her eyes widened, even as they flashed with temper. "How *dare* you try to play the wronged party, you *lying, cheating, sonofa*—"

Either she ran out of adjectives, or she suddenly realized that insulting a man was no way to gain entry into his home.

He lifted an eyebrow. "You were saying?"

His mild tone seemed to enrage her further, though to her credit, she managed to swallow whatever additional words trembled on her tongue. Was it bad of him to remember that small pink tongue wetting his— Oh, hell. Now *he* was the one who pulled up short. Nothing stood to be gained by indulging in a sentimental stroll down memory lane.

No tongues. No nothing.

She licked her lips and took a deep, visible breath. "Samson Oil is trying to buy the Peyton ranch."

Two

Lucy was diabetic; she'd been diagnosed as a twelve-year-old. If she didn't take her insulin, she sometimes got the shakes. But nothing like this. Facing the man she had come to see made her tremble from head to toe. And she couldn't seem to stop. No amount of medicine in the world was ever going to cure her fascination with the ornery, immoral, two-faced, spectacularly handsome Jeff Hartley.

At the moment, however, he was her only hope.

"May I come in?" she asked, trying not to notice the way he smelled of leather and lime and warm male skin.

Jeff stared at her long enough to make her think he might actually say no. In the end, however, gentlemanly manners won out. "Ten minutes," he said gruffly. "I have plans later."

If he meant to wound her, his barb was successful…though she would never give him the satisfaction of knowing for sure. As they navigated the few steps into his living room and sat down, she found herself swamped with memories. This old farmhouse dated back three generations. It had been lovingly cared for and well preserved.

For one brief second, everything came crashing back: the hours she had spent in this bright, cheerful home, the master bedroom upstairs with the queen-size mattress and double-wedding-ring quilt, the bed Jeff had complained was too small for his six-foot-two frame…

She didn't want to remember. Not at all. Not even the spot in this very room where Jeff Hartley had gone down on one knee and offered her a ring and his heart.

Dredging up reserves of audacity and courage, she ignored the past and cut to the chase. "My cousin is trying to sell his land to Samson Oil." Recently, the outsider company had begun buying up acreage in Royal, Texas, at an alarming rate.

Jeff sat back in a leather armchair and hitched one ankle across the opposite knee, drawing attention to his feet. "Is it a fair offer?"

Nobody Lucy had ever known wore scuffed, hand-tooled cowboy boots as well as Jeff Hartley. At one time she wondered if he slept in the damned things. But then came that memorable evening when he showed her how a woman could take off a man's boots at the end of the day...

Her face heated. She jerked her thoughts back to the present. "More than fair. But that's not the point. The property has been in the Peyton family for almost a century. The farmland has contributed to Maverick County's food supply for decades. Equally important—the wildlife preserve was my grandfather's baby. Samson Oil will ruin everything."

"Why does Kenny want to sell?"

"He's sick of farming. He swears there's nothing for him in Royal anymore. He's decided to move to LA and try for an acting career. He pointed out that I sold most of my share to him, left for college and then stayed away. He wants his chance. But he needs cash."

"And this is my problem, how?"

Three

Lucy bit her lip until she tasted blood in her mouth. She couldn't afford to let Jeff goad her into losing her temper. It had happened far too easily on his front porch a moment ago. Her only focus right now should be on getting what she needed to stop a bad, bad decision.

It might have helped if Jeff had gotten old and fat in the past two years. But unfortunately, he looked better than ever. Dark blond hair in need of a trim. Piercing green eyes, definitely on the hostile side. And a long, lean body and lazy gait that made grown women sigh with delight whenever he sauntered by.

"I need you to loan me twenty thousand dollars," she blurted out. "The farm is self-supporting, but Kenny doesn't have a lot of liquid assets. He may be bluffing. Even if he's serious, though, twenty grand will get him off my back and send him on his way. He thinks the only choice he has for coming up with relocation funds is to unload the farm, but I'm trying to give him another option."

"What will happen to the farm when he goes to the West Coast?"

It was a good question. And one she had wrestled with ever since Kenny told her he wanted to leave town. "I suppose I'll have to come back to Royal and take over. At least until Kenny crashes and burns in California and decides to return home."

"You don't have much faith in him, do you?"

She shrugged. "Our fathers were brothers. So we share DNA. But Kenny has always had a problem with focus. Six months ago he wanted to go to vet school. Six months before that he was studying to take the LSAT."

"But you already have a career…right? As a physical trainer? In Austin? That fancy master's degree you earned in sports medicine won't do you much good out on the farm." He didn't even bother to hide the sarcasm.

She wanted to squirm, but she concentrated on breathing in and breathing out, relaxing her muscles one set at a time. "Fortunately, mine is the kind of job that's in demand. I'm sure they won't hold my exact position, but there will be plenty of similar spots when I go back."

"How long do you think you'll have to stay here in Royal?"

"A few months. A year at the most. Will you loan me the money, or not?"

Jeff scowled. "You've got a lot of balls coming to me for help, Lucy."

"You *owe* me," she said firmly. "And you know it." This man...this beautiful, rugged snake of a man had been responsible for the second worst day of her life.

He sat up and leaned forward, resting his elbows on his knees. His veneer of calm peeled away, leaving a male who was a little bit frightening. Dark emerald eyes judged her and found her wanting. "I don't *owe* you a single damn thing. You're the one who walked out on our wedding and made me a laughingstock in Royal."

She jumped to her feet, heart pounding. Lord, he made her mad. "Because I caught you at our rehearsal dinner kissing the maid of honor," she yelled.

Four

Something about Lucy's meltdown actually made Jeff feel a little bit better about this confrontation. At least she wasn't indifferent.

"Sit down, Lucy," he said firmly. "If money is going to change hands, I have two conditions."

She did sit, but the motion looked involuntary…as if her knees gave out. "Conditions?"

"It's a lot of money. And besides, why ask me? Me, of all people?"

"You're rich," she said bluntly, her stormy gaze daring him to disagree.

It was true. His bank account was healthy. And sadly, Lucy had no family to turn to, other than her cousin. Lucy's parents and Kenny's had been killed in a boating accident eight years ago. Because of that tragedy, Lucy had a closer relationship with her cousin than one might expect. They were more like siblings, really.

"If my bottom line is good, it's partly because I don't toss money out the window on a whim."

"It wouldn't be a whim, Jeff. I know the way you think. This thing with Samson Oil is surely eating away at you. *Outsiders*. Taking over land that represents the history of Royal. And then doing God knows what with it. Drilling for oil that isn't there. Selling off the dud acres. Shopping malls. Big box stores. Admit it. The thought makes you shudder. You have to be suspicious about why a mysterious oil company is suddenly trying to buy land that was checked for oil years ago."

That was the problem with old girlfriends. They knew a man's weaknesses. "You're not wrong," he said slowly, taken aback that she had pegged him so well. "But in that case, why wouldn't I buy Kenny's land outright? And make sure that it retains its original purpose?"

"Because it's not the honorable thing to do. Kenny will see the light one day soon. And he would be devastated to come back to Royal and have nothing. Besides, that would be a whole lot more money. Twenty thousand is chicken feed to you."

Jeff grimaced. "You must know some damn fine chickens."

Perhaps she understood him better than he wanted to admit, because after laying out her case, she sat quietly, giving him time to sort through the possibilities. Lucy stared at him with hazel eyes that reflected wariness and a hint of grief.

He felt the grief, too. Had wallowed in it for weeks. But a man had to move on with his life. At one time, he'd been absolutely sure he would grow old with this woman. Now he could barely look at her.

"I need to think about it," he said.

Lucy's temper fired again. "Since when do you have trouble making decisions?" Her hands twisted together in her lap as if she wanted to wrap them around his neck.

"Don't push me, Lucy." He scowled at her. "I'll pick you up out at the farm at five. We'll have dinner, and I'll give you my answer."

Her throat worked. "I don't want to be seen with you."

Five

The barb wasn't unexpected, but it took Jeff's breath momentarily. "The feeling is mutual," he growled. "I'll make reservations in Midland. We'll discuss my terms."

"But that's fifty miles away."

Her visible dismay gave him deep masculine satisfaction. It was time for some payback. Lucy deserved to twist in the wind for what she had done to him. A man's pride was everything.

"Take it or leave it," he said, the words curt.

"I thought you had plans later."

"You let me worry about my calendar, sweetheart."

He watched her flinch at his overt sarcasm. For a moment, he was ashamed of baiting her. But he shored up his anger. Lucy deserved his antagonism and more.

The silence grew in length and breadth, thick with unspoken emotions. If he listened hard enough, he thought he might even be able to hear the rapid beat of her heart. Like a defenseless animal trapped in a cage of its own making.

"Lucy?" He lifted an eyebrow. "I don't have all day."

"You could write me a check this instant," she protested. "Why make me jump through hoops?"

"Maybe because I can."

He was being a bastard. He knew it. And by the look on Lucy's face, she knew it, as well. But the opportunity to make her bend to his will was irresistible.

The fact that each of them could still elicit strong emotions from the other should have been a red flag. But then again, that was the story of their relationship. Though he and Lucy had grown up in the same town, they hadn't really known each other. Not until she'd come home to Royal for a lengthy visit after college graduation.

Lucy's parents had been dead by then. Instead of bunking with her cousin Kenny, Lucy had stayed with her childhood friend and college roommate, Kirsten. One of Kirsten's friends had thrown a hello-to-summer bash, and that's where Jeff had met the luscious Lucy.

He still remembered the moment she'd walked into the room. It was a case of instant lust…at least on his part. She was exactly the kind of woman he liked… tall, confident, and with a wicked sense of humor. The two of them had found a private corner and flirted for three hours.

A week later, they'd ended up in bed together.

Unfortunately, their whirlwind courtship and speedy five-month trip to the altar had ended in disaster. Ironically, if they had followed through with their wedding, two days from now would have been their anniversary.

Did Lucy realize the bizarre coincidence?

She stood up and walked to the foyer. "I have to go." The words were tossed over her shoulder, as if she couldn't wait to get out of his house.

He shrugged and followed her, putting a hand high on the door to keep her from escaping. "I don't want to make a trip out to the farm for nothing. So don't try standing me up. If you want the money, you'll get it on my terms or not at all."

Six

Lucy hurried to her car, heartsick and panicked. Why had she ever thought she could appeal to Jeff Hartley's sense of right and wrong? The man was a scoundrel. She was so angry with herself…angry for approaching him in the first place, and even angrier that apparently she was still desperately in love with him…despite everything he had done.

During the past two years, she had firmly purged her emotional system of memories connected to Jeff Hartley. Never once did she think of the way his arms pulled her tight against his broad chest. Or the silkiness of his always rumpled hair. At night in bed, she surely didn't remember how wonderful it was to feel him slide on top of her and into her, their breath mingling in ragged gasps and groans of pleasure.

Stupid man. She parked haphazardly at the farm and went in search of her cousin. She found him in the barn repairing a harness.

Kenny looked up when she entered. "Hey, Luce. What's up?"

She plopped down on a bale of hay. "How much would it take for you not to sell the land?"

He frowned. "What do you mean? Are you trying to buy it for yourself?"

"Gosh, no. I'd be a terrible farmer. But I have a gut feeling you'll change your mind down the road. And I'm willing to keep things running while you sow your wild oats. So I'm asking...would twenty grand be enough to bankroll your move to LA and get you started? It would be a loan. You'd have to pay back half eventually, and I'll pay back the other half as a thank-you for not letting go of Peyton land."

The frown grew deeper. "A loan from whom?"

Kenny might pretend to be a goofball when it suited him, but the boy was smart...and he knew his grammar.

"From a friend of mine," she said. "No big deal."

Kenny perched on the bale of hay beside hers and put an arm around her shoulders. "What have you done, Luce?"

She sniffed, trying not to cry. "Made a deal with the devil?"

"Are you asking me or telling me?"

Kenny was two years younger than she was. Most of the time she felt like his mother. But for the moment, it was nice to have someone to lean on. "I think Jeff Hartley is going to loan it to me."

"Hell, no." Kenny jumped to his feet, raking both hands through his hair agitatedly. "The man cheated on you and broke your heart. I won't take his money. We'll think of something else. Or I'll convince you it's okay to sell the farm."

"You'll never convince me of that. What if being an actor doesn't pan out?"

"Do you realize how patronizing you sound, Luce? No offense, but what I want to do is more serious than *sowing wild oats*."

She rubbed her temples with her fingertips. "I shouldn't have said that. I'm sorry."

After a few moments, he went back to repairing the harness. "Why did you go to Jeff, Lucy? Why him?"

Bowing her head, she let the tears fall. "The day after tomorrow would have been our wedding anniversary. Jeff Hartley still owes me for that."

Seven

Jeff made arrangements to have the Hartley Ranch covered, personnel wise, in the event that he didn't return from Midland right away. There was no reason in the world to think that he and Lucy might end up in bed together, but he was a planner. A former Boy Scout. Preparation was second nature to him.

As he went about his business, his mind raced on a far more intimate track. Lucy had betrayed the wedding vows she and Jeff had both written. Before they'd ever made it to the altar. And yet she thought Jeff was the one at fault. Even from the perspective of two years down the road, he was still angry about that.

At four o'clock, he showered and quickly packed a bag. He traveled often for cattle shows and other business-related trips, so he was accustomed to the drill.

Then he went online and ordered a variety of items and had them delivered to his favorite hotel.

When he was satisfied that his plans were perfectly in order, he loaded the car, stopped by the bank, and then drove out to the farm. There was at least a fifty-fifty chance Lucy would shut the door in his face. But he was convinced her request for a loan was legit. In order to get the cash, she had to go along with his wishes.

Unfortunately, Kenny answered the door. And he was spoiling for a fight.

Jeff had spent his entire life in Texas. He was no stranger to brawls and the occasional testosterone overload. But if he had plans for himself and Lucy, first he had to get past her gatekeeper. He held up his hands in the universal gesture for noncombative behavior. "I come in peace, big guy."

"Luce never should have asked you for the money. I can manage on my own."

"In LA? I don't think so. Not without liquidating your assets. And that will break your cousin's heart. Is that really what you want to do?"

"You're hardly the man to talk about breaking Lucy's heart." But it was said without heat. As if Kenny understood that more was at stake here than his would-be career.

"Where is she?" Jeff asked. "We need to go."

"I think she was on the phone, but she'll be out soon. Though I sure as hell don't know why."

"Lucy and I have some unfinished business from two years ago. It's time to settle a few scores."

Kenny blanched. "I don't want to be in the middle of this."

"Too late. You shouldn't have tried to sell your land to Samson Oil. And besides, Lucy came to me…not the other way around. What does that tell you?"

Kenny bristled. "It tells me that my cousin cares about me. I have no idea what it says about you."

Eight

Lucy stood just out of sight in the hallway and listened to the two men argue. Strangely, there was not much real anger in the exchange. At one time, Kenny and Jeff had been good friends. Kenny was supposed to walk Lucy down the aisle and hand her over to the rancher who had swept her off her feet. But that moment never happened.

Lucy cleared her throat and eased past Kenny to step onto the porch. "Don't worry if I'm late," she said.

Kenny tugged her wrist and leaned in to kiss her on the cheek. "Text me and let me know your plans. So I don't worry."

His droll attempt to play mother hen made her smile. "Very funny. But yes… I'll be in touch."

At last she had to face Jeff. He stood a few feet

away, his expression inscrutable. In a dark tailored suit, with a crisp white dress shirt and blue patterned tie, he looked like a man in charge of his domain. A light breeze ruffled his hair.

His sharp, intimate gaze scanned her from head to toe. "Let's go" was all he said.

Lucy sighed inwardly. So much for her sexy black cocktail dress with spaghetti straps. The daring bodice showcased her cleavage nicely. Big surly rancher barely seemed to notice.

They descended the steps side by side, Jeff's hand on her elbow. He helped her into the car, closed her door and went around to slide into the driver's seat. The car was not one she remembered. But it had all the bells and whistles. It smelled of leather and even more faintly, the essence of the man himself.

For the first ten miles silence reigned. Pastures of cattle whizzed by outside the window, their existence so commonplace, Lucy couldn't pretend a deep interest in the scenery. Instead, she kicked off her shoes, curled her legs beneath her, and leaned forward to turn on the satellite radio.

"Do you mind?" she asked.

Jeff shot her a glance. "Does being alone with me make you nervous, Lucy?"

"Of course not." Her hand hovered over the knob. More than anything else, she wanted music to fill the awkward silence. But if Jeff saw that as a sign of weakness, then she wouldn't do it.

She sat back, biting her bottom lip. Now the silence was worse. Before, they had simply been two near strangers riding down the road. Jeff's deliberately provocative question set her nerves on edge.

"While we're on our way," she said, "why don't you tell me what these conditions are? The ones I have to agree to so you'll loan me the money?"

Jeff didn't answer her question. "I'm curious. Why doesn't Kenny go out and get his own loan?"

"He's shoveled everything he has back into the farm. His credit's maxed out. Besides, his solution is selling to Samson Oil. I explained that."

"True. You did."

"So tell me, Jeff. What do you want from me?"

Nine

What do you want from me? Lucy's frustrated question was one Jeff would have been glad to answer. In detail. Slowly. All night. But first there were hurdles to jump.

Though he kept his hands on the wheel and his eyes on the road, he had already memorized every nuance of his companion's appearance. Everything from her sexy black high heels all the way up to her sleek and shiny hair tucked behind one ear.

Her black cocktail dress, at first glance, was entirely appropriate for dinner in the big city. But damned if he wasn't going to have the urge to take off his jacket and wrap her up in it. He didn't want other men looking at her.

He felt possessive, which was ridiculous, because

Lucy was definitely her own woman. If she chose to prance stark naked down Main Street, he couldn't stop her. So maybe he needed to take a different tack entirely. Instead of bossing her around, perhaps he should use another very enjoyable means of communication.

Right now, she was a hen with ruffled feathers. He had upset her already. The truth was, he didn't care. He'd rather have anger from Lucy than outright indifference.

He could work with anger.

"We'll talk about the specifics over dinner, Lucy. Why don't you relax and tell me about your work in Austin."

His diversion worked for the next half hour. In his peripheral vision, he watched as Lucy's body language went from tense and guarded to normal. Or at least as normal as it could be given the history between them.

Later, when he pulled up in front of the luxury hotel in the heart of the city, Lucy shot him a sharp-eyed glance.

He took her elbow and led her inside. "The restaurant here is phenomenal," he said. "I think you'll enjoy it."

Over appetizers and drinks, Lucy thawed further. "So far, I'm impressed. I forgot to eat lunch today, so I was starving."

Jeff was hungry, too, but he barely tasted the food. He was gambling a hell of a lot on the outcome of this encounter.

They ordered the works…filet and lobster. With spinach salad and crusty rolls. Clearly, Lucy enjoyed her meal. *He* enjoyed the fact that she didn't fuss about calories and instead ate with enthusiasm.

Good food prepared from fresh ingredients was a sensual experience. It tapped into some of the same pleasure centers as lovemaking. It was hard to bicker under the influence of a really exceptional Chablis and a satisfying, special-occasion dinner.

That's what he was counting on…

Lucy declined dessert. Jeff did, as well. As they lingered over coffee, he could practically see her girding her loins for battle.

She stirred a single packet of sugar into her cup and sat back in her chair, eyeing him steadily. "Enough stalling, Jeff. I've come here with you for dinner, which was amazing, I might add. But I need to have your answer. Will you loan me the money, and what are your conditions?"

Ten

Lucy was braced for bad news. It was entirely possible that Jeff had brought her here—wined and dined her—in order to let her down gently. To give her an outright no.

Watching him take a sip of coffee was only one of many mistakes she had made tonight. When his lips made contact with the rim of his thin china cup, she was almost sure the world stood still for a split second. The man had the most amazing mouth. Firm lips that could caress a woman's breast or kiss her senseless in the space of a heartbeat.

Though it had been two long years, Lucy still remembered the taste of his tongue on hers.

"Jeff?" She heard the impatience in her voice. "I asked you a question."

He nodded slowly. "Okay. Hear me out before you run screaming from the room."

Her nape prickled. "I don't understand."

Leaning toward her, he rested his forearms on the table, hands clasped in front of him. His dark gaze captured hers like a mesmerist. "When you walked out the night before our wedding, we never had closure. I went from being almost married to drastically single so fast it's a wonder I didn't get whiplash."

"What's your point?" Her throat was tight.

"Divorced couples end up back in bed together all the time. Lovers break up and hook up and break up again. I'm curious to see if you and I still have a spark."

Hyperventilation threatened. "We can talk about that later." *Much later.* "You said you had two conditions. What are they?" For the first time tonight, she caught a glimpse of something in his eyes. Was it pain? Or vulnerability? Not likely.

He shrugged. "I want you to ask Kirsten to tell you what really happened that night."

"I don't need to talk to Kirsten. I'm not blind. I saw everything. You kissed her and she kissed you back. Both of you betrayed me. The truth is, Kirsten and I have barely spoken since that night. She has shut me out. I think she's embarrassed that she didn't stop you."

"And you really believe that?"

His tone wasn't sarcastic. If anything, the words were wistful, cajoling. She'd spent two horrid years wondering why the man who professed to love her madly had been such a jerk. Or why Kirsten, her best friend, hadn't punched Jeff in the stomach. She had seen Kirsten's face when Lucy caught them. The other woman had looked shattered. But her arms had definitely been twined about Jeff's neck.

"I don't know what to believe anymore," she muttered. Jeff hadn't dated anyone at all in the last twenty-four months according to Royal's gossipy grapevine. He was a young, virile man in his prime. If he was such a lying, cheating scoundrel, why hadn't he been out on the town with a dozen women in the interim? "And if I do go talk to Kirsten about what happened? That's it? What about the other requirement?"

Those chiseled lips curved upward in a smile that made her spine tighten and her stomach curl. "I'd like the two of us to go upstairs and spend the night together."

Eleven

Go upstairs and spend the night together.

His words echoed in her brain like tiny pinballs. "You mean sex?"

Jeff laughed out loud, but it was gentle laughter, and his eyes were filled with warmth. "Yes, Lucy. Sex. I've missed you. I've missed us."

Oh, my...

What was a woman supposed to say to that kind of proposition? Especially when it sounded so very appealing. She cleared her throat. "If you're offering to pay me twenty thousand dollars to have sex with you, I think we could both get arrested."

His smile was enigmatic. "Let's not muddy the waters, then. I promise to give you the money for Kenny as long as you have a conversation with Kirsten." He reached across the table and took one of her hands in both of his. When he rubbed his thumb across her wrist, it was all she could do not to jerk away in a panic.

"Steady, Lucy." His grip tightened. "I think deep in your heart you know the truth. But you're afraid to face it. I understand that. Maybe it will take time. So for tonight, I'm not expecting you to make any sweeping declarations. I'm only asking if you'll be my lover again. One night. For closure. Unless you change your mind and decide you want more."

"Why would I do that?" she asked faintly, remembering all the evenings she had cried herself to sleep.

"You'll have to figure it out for yourself," he said. That same thumb rubbed back and forth across her knuckles.

She seized on one inescapable truth. "But I don't have anything with me to stay overnight," she said, grasping at straws. "And neither do you."

"I brought a bag," he replied calmly. "And I ordered a few items for a female companion. I believe you'll find I've thought of everything you need to be comfortable."

"And you don't think this is at all creepy?" With her free hand she picked up her water glass, intending to take a sip. But her fingers shook so much she set it back down immediately.

Jeff released her, his expression sober. "You're the one who came to see me, not the other way around. If you want me to take you home, all you have to do is say so. But I'm hoping you'll give us this one night to see if the spark is still there."

"Why are you doing this?" she whispered. He was breaking her heart all over again, and she was so damned afraid to trust him. Even worse, she was afraid to trust herself.

Jeff summoned the waiter and dealt with the check. Moments later, the transaction was complete. Jeff stood and held out his hand. "I need your decision, Lucy." He was tall and sexy and clear-eyed in his resolve. "Shall we go, or shall we stay? It's up to you. It always has been."

Twelve

Jeff's heartbeat thundered in his chest. He wasn't usually much of a gambler, but he was betting on a future that, at the moment, didn't exist.

It was a thousand years before Lucy slid her small hand into his bigger one. "Yes," she said. The word was barely audible.

He led her among the crowded tables and out into the hotel foyer. After tucking her into an elegant wingback chair, he brushed a finger across her cheek. "Stay here. I won't be long."

Perhaps the desk clerk thought him a tad weird. Jeff could barely register for glancing back over his shoulder to see if Lucy had bolted. But all was well. She had her phone in her hand and was apparently checking messages.

When he had the key, he went back for her. "Ready?"

Her face was pale when she looked up at him. But she smiled and rose to her feet. "Yes."

They shared an elevator with three other people. On the seventh floor, Jeff took Lucy's arm and steered her off. "This way," he said gruffly as he located their room number on the brass placard. They were at the end of the hall, far from the noise of the elevator and the ice machine.

He'd booked a suite. Inside the pleasantly neutral sitting room, he took off his jacket and tie. "Would you like more wine?" he asked.

Lucy hovered by the door. "No. Why do you want me to go talk to Kirsten?" Her eyes were huge…perhaps revealing distress over the shambles of their past.

He leaned against the arm of the sofa. "She was your friend from childhood. You and I had dated less than a year. As angry as I was with you, on some level I understood."

"Why were you angry with *me*?" she asked, her expression bewildered. "You were the one who cheated."

He didn't rise to the bait. "It's been two years, Lucy. Two long, frustrating years when you and I should have been starting our life together. Surely you've had time enough to figure it out by now."

"You didn't come after me." Her voice was small, the tone wounded.

Ah…there it was. The evidence of his own stupidity. "You're right about that. I let my pride get in the way. When you wouldn't take my calls, I wanted to make you grovel. But as it turns out, that was an abysmally arrogant and unproductive attitude on my part. I'm sorry I didn't follow you back to Austin. I should have. Maybe one good knock-down, drag-out fight would have cleared the air."

"And now…if I agree to go talk to Kirsten?"

He swallowed the last of his wine and set the glass aside. "I don't want to discuss Kirsten anymore. You and I are the only two people here in this suite. What I desperately need is make love to you."

Thirteen

Lucy sucked in a deep breath, her insides tumbling as they had the one and only time she rode the Tilt-A-Whirl at the county fair. On that occasion, she had tossed her cookies afterward.

Tonight was different. Tonight, the butterflies were all about anticipation and arousal and the rebirth of hope. Why else would she be here with Jeff Hartley?

She nodded, kicking off her shoes. "Yes." There were a million words she wanted to say to him, and not all of them kind. But for some reason, the only thing that mattered at this very moment was feeling the warmth of his skin beneath her fingers one more time.

She felt more emotionally bereft than brave, but she made her feet move…carrying her across the plush carpet until she stood face-to-face with Jeff. His gaze was stormy, his fists were clenched at his sides.

He stared into her eyes as if looking for something he was afraid he wouldn't find. "God, you're beautiful," he said, his voice hoarse. "I thought I could put you out of my mind, but that was laughable. You've haunted every room in my house. Kiss me, Lucy."

With one of his strong arms around her back, binding her to him, she went up on her tiptoes and found his mouth with hers. The taste of him brought tears to sting her eyelids, but she blinked them back, wanting this moment to be about light and warmth and pleasure. He held her gently as he took everything she thought she knew and stripped it away, leaving only a yearning that was heart-deep and visceral.

She wanted to say something, but Jeff was a man possessed. He found the zipper at her back and lowered it with one smooth move. Then he shimmied the garment down her body and held her arm as she stepped out of the small heap of fabric.

Beneath the dress, she wore lacy underthings. Jeff didn't pause to admire them. The lingerie went the way of the crumpled dress.

Suddenly, she realized that she was completely naked, and her would-be lover was staring. Hotly. Glassy-eyed. As if he'd been struck in the head and was seeing stars.

She crossed her arms over strategic areas and scowled. "Take off your clothes, Mr. Hartley. This show works both ways."

If the situation hadn't been so emotionally fraught,

she might have chuckled when Jeff dragged his shirt, still half-buttoned, over his head. His pants and socks and shoes were next in the frenzied disrobing.

Underneath, he wore snug-fitting black boxers that strained to contain his arousal. Suddenly, she felt shy and afraid and clueless. Had she ever really known this man at all?

He didn't give her time for second thoughts. "We'll be more comfortable on the bed," he promised, scooping her up and carrying her through the adjacent doorway. She barely noticed the furnishings or the color scheme. Her gaze was locked on Jeff's face.

His cheekbones were slashed with color. His eyes glittered with lust. "You're mine, Lucy."

Fourteen

The bottom dropped out of her stomach. It was as simple as that. Even if he hadn't said the words, she would have felt his deep conviction in the way he moved his hands over her body.

He still wore his underwear, maybe to keep things from rushing along too rapidly. He was tanned all over from his days of working in the hot sun. His chest was a work of art, sleekly muscled…lightly dusted with golden hair.

Even as she took in the magnificence that was Jeff Hartley, she couldn't help but question his motives. As a rancher and a member of the Texas Cattleman's Club in Royal, he was a well-respected member of the community. Had his reputation suffered when she walked out on him? Was there a part of him that wanted revenge?

He loomed over her on one elbow, his emerald eyes darker than normal, his forehead damp, his skin hot. It was all she could do to be still and let him map her curves like a blind man. Need rose, hot and tormenting, between her clenched thighs.

How could she want him so desperately while knowing full well there were serious unresolved issues between them? "Jeff," she whispered, not really knowing what to say. "Please…" Despite what her head told her, her heart and her body were in control.

It was as if they had never been apart. He rolled her to her stomach and moved aside a swath of her hair to kiss the nape of her neck. The press of his lips against sensitive skin sent sparkles of sensation all down to her feet.

When he nibbled his way along her spine, her hands grabbed the sheets. He lay heavy against her, his big body weighing her down deliciously.

At last she felt him move away. He scrambled out of his boxers and rolled her to face him once again. She let her arms fall lax above her head, enjoying the way his avid gaze scoured her from head to toe.

It had been two years since she had seen him naked…two years since she had seen him at all. Beginning with what would have been their wedding morning, he had phoned her every single day for a week. Each one of those times she had let his call go to voice mail, telling herself he should have had the guts to face her in person.

Had she wronged him grievously? In her blind hurt, had she rushed to judgment? The enormity of the question made her head spin.

For weeks and months, she had wallowed in her self-righteous anger, calling Jeff Hartley every dirty name in the book, telling herself she hated him...that he was a worthless cad, a two-timing player.

But what if she had been wrong? What if she had been terribly, dreadfully wrong?

He used his thumb to erase the frown lines between her brows. "What's the matter, buttercup?"

Hearing the silly nickname made the lump in her throat grow larger. "I don't know what we're doing, Jeff."

His smile was lopsided, more rueful than happy. "Damned if I know either. But let's worry about that tomorrow."

She cupped his cheek, feeling the light stubble of late-day beard. "Since when do *you* channel Scarlett O'Hara?"

Without answering, he reached in his discarded pants for a condom and took care of business. Then he moved between her thighs. "Put your arms around my neck, Lucy. I want to feel you skin to skin."

Fifteen

Jeff tried to live an honorable life. He gave to charity, offered work to those who needed it, supported his local civic organizations and donated large sums of money to the church where he had been baptized as an infant.

But lying in Lucy's arms, on the brink of restaking a claim that had lain dormant for two years, he would have sold his soul to the devil if he could have frozen time.

Lucy's eyes were closed.

"Look at me," he commanded. "I want you to see my face when I take you."

Her breath came in short, sharp pants. She nodded, her eyelids fluttering upward as she obeyed.

Gently, he spread her thighs and positioned his aching flesh against the moist, pink lips of her sex. When he pushed inside, he was pretty sure he blacked out for a moment. *Two years. Two damn years.*

It was everything he remembered and more. The fragrance of her silky skin. The sound of her soft, incoherent cries. His body and his soul would have recognized her even in the dark, anywhere in the world.

He felt her heart beating against his chest. Or maybe it was his heart. It was impossible to separate the two. Burying his face in the crook of her shoulder, he moved in her steadily, sucking in a sharp breath when she wrapped her legs around his waist, driving him deeper.

He thrust slowly at first, but all the willpower in the world couldn't stem the tide of his hunger. His body betrayed him, his desire cresting sharply in a release that left him almost insensate.

Lucy hadn't come. He knew that. But his embarrassment was blunted by the sheer euphoria of being with her again. He kissed her cheek. "I'm sorry, love." He touched her gently, intimately, stroking and teasing until she climaxed, too. Afterward, he held her close for long minutes.

But reality eventually intruded.

Lucy reclined on her elbow, head propped on her hand. "May I ask you a very personal question?"

Though his breathing was still far from steady, he nodded. "Anything."

Lucy reached out and smoothed a lock of his hair. Her gaze was troubled. "When was the last time you had sex?"

Here it was. The first test of their tenuous reconciliation. "You should know," he said quietly. "You were there."

She went white, her expression anguished, tears spilling from her eyes and rolling down her cheeks. "You're lying," she whispered.

Her accusation angered him. But he gathered her into his arms and held her as she sobbed. Two years of grief and separation. Two years of lost happiness.

"I know you don't believe me, Lucy." He combed her hair with his fingers. "Maybe you never will. Don't cry so hard. You'll make yourself sick."

Perhaps they should have talked first. But his need for her had obliterated everything else. Now she was distraught, and he didn't know how to help her get to the truth. Was this going to be the only moment they had? If so, he wasn't prepared to let it end so soon.

Feeling her nude body against his healed the raw places inside him. She was his. He would fight. For however long it took. No matter what happened, he was never letting her go again.

Sixteen

Lucy's brain whirled in sickening circles. Jeff wanted her to believe he hadn't been with another woman since she walked out on him. He expected her to believe he had not cheated on her.

She should have been elated...relieved. Instead, she was shattered and confused and overwhelmed. Was she going to be one of those women who blindly accepted whatever her lover told her? Where was her pride? Her intuition? Her intellect?

Jeff was silent, but tense. She knew him well enough to realize that he was angry. Even so, the strong arms holding her close were her only anchors at a moment when everything she thought she knew was shattering into tiny fragments and swirling away.

At last, the storm of grief passed. She lay against

him limp with emotional distress. Taking a deep breath, she tried to sit up. "We need to go back to Royal. Right now. I need to see you and Kirsten in the same room at the same time to hash this out."

Jeff moved up against the headboard. His jaw was tight, but he scooped her into his lap. "It can wait until tomorrow. We deserve this night together, Lucy. You and I. No one else. Even if you don't believe me."

With her cheek against his chest, she seesawed between hope and despair. Was it possible she hadn't lost him after all, or was she being a credulous fool? If she had placed more trust in what they had from the beginning, it might never have come to this. Was it too late to repair the damage and to reclaim the future that had almost been destroyed?

And what if Jeff *had* initiated the kiss with Kirsten? Could she forgive him and move on? Was what they had worth another chance? Would their relationship ever be the same?

She was deeply moved, unbearably regretful, and at the same time giddy with hope. Tipping back her head so she could see his face, she memorized his features. The heavy-lidded green eyes. The strong chin. The slightly crooked nose. The tiny scar below his left cheekbone.

He gazed down at her with a half-smile. "Are we good?"

"I'm not sure." She wanted to say more. She wanted to pour out her heart...to tell him about the endless months of despair and loneliness. But now was not the time to be sad. "Kiss me again," she whispered unsteadily. "So I know this isn't a dream."

Jeff leaned her over his arm and gave her what she asked for, warm and slow...soft and deep. With each fractured sigh on her part and every ragged groan from him, arousal shimmered and spread until every cell of her body pulsed wildly with wanting him. She grabbed handfuls of his hair, trying to drag him closer.

He winced and laughed. "Easy, darlin'. I don't want to go bald just yet."

His trademark humor was one of the things that had attracted her to him in the beginning. That and his broad-shouldered, lanky body.

Before she knew what was happening, he had levered her onto her back and was leaning over her, shaping the curves of her breasts with his fingertips. Her nipples were so sensitive, she could hardly stand for him to touch them.

"I need you inside me again," she pleaded.

"Not yet." His smile was feral. "Have patience, Lucy, love. We've got all night."

Seventeen

Jeff wanted to worship her body and mark it as his and drive her insane with pleasure. It was a tall order for a man still wrung out from his own release. Not that he wasn't ready for another round. He was. He definitely was. His erection throbbed with a hunger that wouldn't be sated anytime soon.

But somehow he had to make Lucy understand.

When he tasted the tips of her breasts, circled the areolas with his tongue, she gasped and arched her back. He pressed her to the mattress and moved south, teasing her belly button before kissing his way down her hips and thighs and legs one at a time. He even spent a few crazy minutes playing with her toes, and this from a man who had never once entertained a foot fetish.

By this point, she was calling him names…pleading for more.

He laughed, but it was a hoarse laugh. He knew the joke was on him. All his plans to demonstrate how high he could push her evaporated in the driving urge to fill her and erase the memory of every hour that had separated them.

His brain was so fuzzy he only remembered the new condom at the last minute. Once he was ready, he knelt and lifted one of Lucy's legs onto his shoulder. He paused—only a moment—to appreciate the sensual picture she made.

Everything about her was perfect…from the graceful arch of her neck to her narrow waist to the small mole just below her right breast.

He touched her deliberately, stroking the little spot that made her body weep for him. Even though he was gentle and almost lazy in his caress, Lucy climaxed wildly, her release beautiful and real and utterly impossible to resist. "God, I want you," he muttered.

When he thrust inside her, her orgasm hit another peak. The feel of her inner muscles fluttering against his sex drove him to the brink of control. He went still…chest heaving, hips moving restlessly despite his pause.

"Lucy?"

Her teeth dug into her bottom lip. "Yes?"

"I was furious with you for not trusting me. But I never stopped loving you."

"Oh, Jeff…" The look on her face told him she wasn't there yet. She still had doubts. He could wait, maybe. He wanted her to be absolutely sure. For now it was enough to feel…and to know…

Lucy was his.

He retreated and lifted her onto her knees, stuffing pillows beneath her. Her butt was the prettiest thing he'd ever seen, heart-shaped and full. Lucy had bemoaned the curves of her bottom on numerous occasions. Tonight, as he palmed it and squeezed it and steadied himself against it to enter her again with one firm push, he decided he could spend the rest of his life proving to her how perfect it was.

Leaning forward, he gathered her hair into a ponytail, securing it with his fist and using the grip to turn her head. "Look in the mirror, Lucy. This is us. This is real."

Eighteen

Lucy hadn't even noticed that the dresser was conveniently situated across from the bed…and that the mirror faithfully reflected Jeff's sun-bronzed body and her own paler frame. The carnal image was indelibly imprinted on her brain. As long as she lived, she would never forget this moment.

She closed her eyes and bent her head. Jeff released her hair, letting it fall around her face. Behind her, his harsh breathing was audible. At last, he moved with a muffled shout, slamming into her again and again until he shuddered and moaned and slumped on top of her as they both collapsed onto the mattress.

Minutes later…maybe hours, so skewed was her sense of time, she stirred. In the interim, they had untangled their bodies. Jeff lay flat on his back, one arm

flung across his eyes. She snuggled against him, drap-
ing her leg across his hairy thigh. "Are you alive?"

"Mmph…"

It wasn't much of a response, but it made her smile.

She danced her fingertips over his rib cage. At one
time, he had been very ticklish.

His face scrunched up and he batted her hand away.
"Five minutes," he begged, the words slurred. "That's
all I need."

"Take your time," she teased. She rested her cheek
against his chest, feeling so light with happiness it was
a wonder she didn't float up to the ceiling. Maybe she
was being naive. Maybe he would hurt her again. But
at the moment, none of that seemed to matter.

"You never gave me a chance to explain two years
ago," he muttered.

His statement dampened her euphoria. "Would it
have mattered? I was desperately hurt and in shock. I'm
not sure anything you said would have gotten through
to me."

"I deserved a fair hearing, Lucy. We were in a committed relationship, but you were too stubborn to be
reasonable."

His eyes were closed, so she couldn't see his expression. But his jaw was tight.

Was it all an act? Jeff playing up his innocence?

There was only one way to know for sure, even if
the prospect curled her stomach. "Will you do me a
favor?" she asked quietly.

Jeff yawned. "The way I feel right now, you could

ask me for the moon and I'd call NASA to help me get it for you."

She reared up on one elbow and gaped. "Why, Jeff Hartley! That was the most romantic thing you've ever said to me."

And there it was again. *Doubt.* Many a woman had been swayed by pretty words.

He chuckled, holding her tightly against his side. "I've had two years to practice," he said. "Prepare to be amazed. But let's not get off track. What's this big favor you need from me?"

"Will you go with me to Kirsten's house?"

His entire body froze. "If it's all the same to you, I'd rather not come anywhere near that woman."

She kissed his bicep. "Please. I have to hear the truth. I know you want me to take you on faith, but I need something more concrete. I need you to understand my doubts, and I need your moral support."

"Damn it. That's what I get for promising you the moon."

Nineteen

The following morning when Lucy woke up, she didn't know where she was. And then it all came back to her in a rush of memories from the night before. She and Jeff Hartley had done naughty things in this huge bed. Naughty, wonderful things.

During the night, he had insisted on holding her close as they slept, though in truth, sleep had been far down the list of their favorite activities. Actually, ranking right below mind-blowing sex were the strawberries and champagne they had ordered from room service at 3:00 a.m.

Jeff was still asleep. She studied him unashamedly, feeling her heart swell with hope and then contract with fear. Loving him once had nearly destroyed her. Could she let herself love him again?

She flinched in surprise when the naked man beneath the covers moved and spoke. "I am not a peep show for your private entertainment," he mumbled.

Reaching beneath the sheet, she took him in her hand. "Are you sure?"

What followed was a very pleasant start to their morning. When they were both rumpled and limp with satisfaction, she poked his arm. "Time to put on some clothes and check out. I want to get this over with."

An hour later, they were on the highway, headed back to Royal. Lucy sat rigid in her seat, her hands clenched in her lap. Layers of dread filled her stomach with each passing mile.

When they reached the fringes of Royal proper, Jeff pulled off on the side of the road and turned to face her. "There's something else I need to tell you."

She blanched. "Oh?"

"Nothing bad," he said hastily, correctly reading her state of mind. "I want you to know that I had my bank transfer twenty thousand dollars to Kenny's account before you and I ever made it to Midland. I wanted you and me to be intimate, but only if you wanted it, too."

Lucy shook her head. "Thank you for that." But even as she said the words, she wondered if his generosity might be a ploy to win her trust…to play the knight in shining armor.

Of course, Jeff knew where Kirsten lived. The party where Jeff and Lucy first connected had been down the street from Kirsten's house. When Jeff parked at the curb, Lucy took a deep breath. "This is it, I guess."

Jeff was at her side as they made their way up the

walk. Lucy rang the bell. Kirsten herself opened the door…and upon seeing Lucy and Jeff together, immediately turned the color of milk, her expression distraught. She didn't invite them in. They stood in an awkward trio with the noonday sun beaming down.

Lucy squared her shoulders. "It's been painful having you treat me so coldly these last two years, Kirsten. But I have to know the truth. If Jeff kissed you and you were seduced into responding, I need to hear you admit it."

Kirsten scowled. "What does the sainted Jeff Hartley have to say about the whole mess? I suppose he's told you what a bitch I am…what a terrible friend."

"Actually, he hasn't said much of anything. The man I knew two years ago wouldn't have cheated on me. But the only other explanation is that my best friend deliberately ruined my wedding."

Kirsten wrapped her arms around her waist, her expression hunted. "Why would I do that?"

"I don't know. But I've run out of scenarios, and I'm damned tired of wondering." Kirsten sneered. "Men are pigs. They want what they can't have. Jeff put the moves on me. He cheated on you."

Suddenly, the pain was as fresh as if the incident had happened yesterday. Seeing Kirsten in Jeff's arms had nearly killed Lucy. But now she had to take one of them on faith. Either her childhood friend or her lover.

She stared at Kirsten. "Did *he* cheat on me? Or did *you*?"

It was a standoff two years in the making. No matter what the answer turned out to be, Lucy lost someone she cared about, someone she loved.

Jeff remained silent during the long, dreadful seconds that elapsed. Time settled into slow motion...

At last, Kirsten's face crumpled. Her eyes flashed with a combination of guilt and anger. "If you'd had more faith in him, nothing I did would have mattered."

Lucy gasped, struck by the truth in the accusation. But her own behavior wasn't on trial at the moment. Shock paralyzed her, despite the part of her that must have accepted the truth somewhere deep down inside. "So it's true?" Lucy spared one glance at Jeff, but he was stone-faced.

Kirsten shrugged. "It's true. Your precious Jeff is innocent."

Lucy trembled. Knowing was one thing. Hearing it bluntly stated out loud was painful...and baffling. "Why, Kirsten? I have to know why?"

Kirsten was almost defiant now. "I was jealous. Ever since we were kids, things seemed so easy for you. When we came back from college and you hooked up with Jeff at the party, I was furious. I'd had my eye on him for a long time."

Lucy shook her head in disbelief. "You were so popular, Kirsten. I don't even know what you mean."

Kirsten shrugged. "I hoarded my resentment. Everything came to a head the night of your rehearsal dinner. I saw my chance and I took it. I kissed Jeff. Because I knew you were right outside the door. He had nothing to do with it."

"Oh, Kirsten. You were my best friend."

The other woman shook her head. "But not anymore." Quietly, Kirsten closed the door.

Twenty

Jeff took Lucy's arm and steered her back toward the car. "Give her time," he said. "The two of you may get beyond this."

Lucy stared at him. "How can you be so calm?"

He caressed her cheek, his eyes filled with warmth. "I have you back in my life again, Lucy. Nothing can hurt me now."

"Take me home with you, Jeff. Please."

They made the trip in silence. Her thoughts were in shambles. How had she been so wrong about so many things?

In Jeff's living room, she prowled. He leaned a shoulder against the doorframe, his gaze following her around the room. At last, he sighed. "Sometimes we have to put the past behind us, sweetheart. We have to choose to be happy and move on."

At last, Lucy stood in front of him, hands on her hips. "I love you, too, Jeff. I'm sorry I didn't trust you… that I didn't trust us. Kirsten had been my friend since we were nine years old. When I saw her in your arms, it didn't make sense. So my default was to doubt you. And maybe to doubt myself, too, because I fell in love with you so quickly." She took a deep breath. "I adore you. I suppose I'll have to spend the rest of my life making this up to you."

He pulled her close and kissed her hard, making her heart skip several beats. "Nonsense. We're not going to talk about it again. Today is our new beginning."

Even in the midst of an almost miraculous second chance, Lucy fretted. "There's one more thing."

He scooped her into his arms and carried her to the sofa, sprawling with her in his arms. "Go ahead," he said, his tone resigned.

"I don't want people to gossip about us. Can we please keep this quiet? At least until after Christmas? That will give me time to go back to Austin and turn in my notice. I'll have to sell my condo if I'm coming back to run the farm. I'll convince Kenny to turn down the Samson Oil offer and stick around until the new year."

Jeff's eyes narrowed…giving him the look of a really pissed off cowboy. "No way," he said, his jaw thrust out. "We're getting married this week. I'm not stupid."

She petted his shirtfront. "Then go with me to Austin," she said urgently. "We'll have a quiet wedding at the courthouse. Just you and me. But nobody has to know. I want time for us to be us." She kissed his chin. "You understand, don't you?"

He moved her beneath him on the sofa, unzipping her black pants and toying with the lacy edge of her undies. "As long as you're in my bed every night, I'll do whatever you want, Lucy. But I won't wait to put my ring on your finger."

She linked her arms around his neck, drawing his head down so she could kiss him. "Whatever you say, cowboy. I'm all yours."

* * * * *

Don't miss a single installment of
TEXAS CATTLEMAN'S CLUB:
LIES AND LULLABIES

*Baby secrets and a scheming
sheikh rock Royal, Texas*

COURTING THE COWBOY BOSS
by USA TODAY *bestselling author Janice Maynard*

LONE STAR HOLIDAY PROPOSAL
by USA TODAY *bestselling author Yvonne Lindsay*

NANNY MAKES THREE
by Cat Schield

THE DOCTOR'S BABY DARE
by USA TODAY *bestselling author Michelle Celmer*

THE SEAL'S SECRET HEIRS
by Kat Cantrell

A SURPRISE FOR THE SHEIKH
by Sarah M. Anderson

IN PURSUIT OF HIS WIFE
by Kristi Gold

A BRIDE FOR THE BOSS
by USA TODAY *bestselling author Maureen Child*

*If you're on Twitter, tell us what you think
of Harlequin Desire! #harlequindesire*

Available December 1, 2015

#2413 BANE
The Westmorelands • by Brenda Jackson
Rancher and military hero Bane Westmoreland is on a mission to reconnect with the one who got away—his estranged wife. And when the beautiful chemist's discovery puts her in danger, Bane vows to protect her at all costs...

#2414 TRIPLETS UNDER THE TREE
Billionaires and Babies • by Kat Cantrell
A plane crash took his memory. But then billionaire fighter Antonio Cavallari makes it home for the holidays only to discover the triplets he never knew...and their very off-limits, very tempting surrogate mother.

#2415 LONE STAR HOLIDAY PROPOSAL
Texas Cattleman's Club: Lies and Lullabies
by Yvonne Lindsay
At risk of losing her business, single mother Raina Patterson finds solace in the arms of Texas deal-maker Nolan Dane. But does this mysterious stranger have a hidden agenda that will put her heart at even bigger risk?

#2416 A WHITE WEDDING CHRISTMAS
Brides and Belles • by Andrea Laurence
When a cynical wedding planner is forced to work with her teenage crush to plan his sister's Christmas wedding, sparks fly! But will she finally find a happily-ever-after of her own with this second-chance man?

#2417 THE RANCHER'S SECRET SON
Lone Star Legends • by Sara Orwig
For wealthy rancher Nick Milan, hearing the woman he loved and lost tell him he's a daddy is the shock of a lifetime. The revelation could derail his political career...or put the real prize back within tantalizing reach...

#2418 TAKING THE BOSS TO BED
by Joss Wood
After producer Ryan Jackson kisses a stranger to save her from his client's unwanted attentions, he realizes she's actually his newest employee! Faking a relationship is now essential for business, but soon real passion becomes the bottom line...

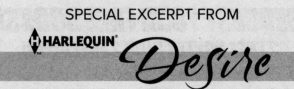
With her heart thundering hard in her chest, Crystal began throwing items in the suitcase open on her bed. Had she imagined it or had she been watched when she'd entered her home tonight? She had glanced around several times and hadn't noticed anything or anyone. But still…

She took a deep breath, knowing she couldn't lose her cool. She made a decision to leave her car here and a few lights burning inside her house to give the impression she was home. She would call a cab to take her to the airport and would take only the necessities and a few items of clothing. She could buy anything else she needed.

But this, she thought as she studied the photo album she held in her hand, went everywhere with her. She had purchased it right after her last phone call with Bane. Her parents had sent Crystal to live with Aunt Rachel to finish out the last year of school. They wanted to get her away from Bane, not knowing she and Bane had secretly married.

A couple of months after she left Denver, she'd gotten a call from him. He'd told her he'd enlisted in the navy because he needed to grow up, become responsible and make something out of himself. She deserved a man who could be all that he could be, and after he'd accomplished that goal he would come for her. Sitting on the edge of the bed now, she flipped through the album, which she had dedicated to Bane. She thought of him often. Every day. What she tried not to think about was why it was taking him so long to come back for her, or how he might be somewhere enjoying life without her. Forcing those thoughts from her mind, she packed the album in her luggage.

Moments later, she had rolled her luggage into the living room and was calling for a cab when her doorbell rang.

She went still. Nobody ever visited her. Who would be doing so now? She crept back into the shadows of her hallway, hoping whoever was at the door would think she wasn't home. She held her breath when the doorbell sounded again. Did the person on the other side know she was there?

She rushed into her bedroom and grabbed her revolver out of the nightstand drawer. By the time she'd made it back to the living room, there was a second knock. She moved toward the door, but stopped five feet away. "Who is it?" She tightened her hands on the revolver.

There was a moment of silence. And then a voice said, "It's me, Crystal. Bane."

Bane will do whatever it takes to keep his woman safe, but will it be enough?

Don't miss BANE by New York Times *bestselling author Brenda Jackson. Available December 2015 wherever Harlequin® Desire books and ebooks are sold.*

www.Harlequin.com